Death of a Liar
Death of a Policeman
Death of Yesterday
Death of a Kingfisher
Death of a Chimney Sweep
Death of a Valentine
Death of a Witch
Death of a Gentle Lady
Death of a Maid
Death of a Dreamer
Death of a Bore
Death of a Poison Pen
Death of a Village
Death of a Celebrity
Death of a Dustman
Death of an Addict
Death of a Scriptwriter
Death of a Dentist
Death of a Macho Man
Death of a Nag
Death of a Charming Man
Death of a Travelling Man

Death of a Greedy Woman
Death of a Prankster
Death of a Snob
Death of a Hussy
Death of a Perfect Wife
Death of an Outsider
Death of a Cad
Death of a Gossip
A Highland Christmas

M. C. BEATON

Death *of a* Nurse

GC

GRAND CENTRAL
PUBLISHING

LARGE PRINT

Grand Central Publishing
Hachette Book Group
1290 Avenue of the Americas
New York, NY 10104

www.HachetteBookGroup.com

Printed in the United States of America

RRD-C

First Edition: February 2016
10 9 8 7 6 5 4 3 2 1

Grand Central Publishing is a division of Hachette Book Group, Inc.
The Grand Central Publishing name and logo is a trademark of Hachette Book Group, Inc.

The Hachette Speakers Bureau provides a wide range of authors for speaking events. To find out more, go to www.hachettespeakersbureau.com or call (866) 376-6591.

The publisher is not responsible for websites (or their content) that are not owned by the publisher.

Library of Congress Cataloging-in-Publication Data has been applied for.

ISBN 978-1-4555-5825-4 (hardcover)
ISBN 978-1-4555-3632-0 (large print)

This book is dedicated to all the Tapping family:
Dave, Zoe, Rachael, Matthew
and last, but not least, Harry.
With affection.

Death *of a* Nurse

Chapter One

I wish I loved the Human Race;
I wish I loved its silly face;
I wish I liked the way it walks;
I wish I liked the way it talks:
And when I'm introduced to one
I wish I thought What Jolly Fun!

—Sir Walter A. Raleigh

Police Sergeant Hamish Macbeth was in a sour mood, despite the sunny, windy weather. His new sidekick, policeman Charlie Carter, was giving him claustrophobia. Admittedly, Charlie was kind and amiable and worked hard. But he was big, very big. Hamish was tall but Charlie was taller and broader, and he was clumsy. He fell over the furniture, he broke china and glass, and when Hamish shouted at him, he looked so miserable that Hamish immediately felt guilty.

Hamish's odd-looking dog called Lugs walked at his heels as did his wild cat, Sonsie. Wild cats are an endangered species and Hamish was always afraid that Sonsie would be taken away. As if sensing his master's bad mood, Lugs looked up at Hamish with his strange blue eyes.

The breeze sent sunny ripples dancing across the sea loch. The village of Lochdubh in Sutherland looked like a picture postcard with its row of small eighteenth-century white-washed cottages facing the sea loch. Hamish was leaning on the seawall, thinking dark thoughts about getting Charlie transferred back to Strathbane, that ghastly town full of drugs and crime.

He turned away from the wall, and that was when he saw a vision. A nurse came tripping along with a shopping basket over her arm.

From her jaunty cap to her candy-striped dress and her black stockings, she looked like a fantasy nurse. She went into Patel's grocery store and Hamish followed. He waited outside until she emerged with a basket full of groceries over her arm. He swept off his cap. "May I carry your messages for you?"

She smiled up at him from a perfect oval of a face. Her large eyes were grey and fringed with heavy lashes. Her hair, under the cap, was fair and glossy.

"Thank you," she said. "But my car is right there."

"I'll put them in the boot for you," said Hamish. "Do you work near here?"

"Yes, I am a private nurse. I take care of old Mr. Harrison."

"He lives in that old hunting lodge out on the Braikie road," said Hamish. "But he had a nurse, a Miss Macduff."

She laughed. "He fired her and employed me. So you're the local copper."

"Hamish Macbeth. And you are?"

"Gloria Dainty."

He put her basket in the boot. She bent over the boot to arrange something and the frisky wind lifted the skirt of her dress, revealing that those stockings were held up with lacy suspenders.

"I'll follow you," said Hamish. "I haven't said hullo to Mr. Harrison." He had actually visited the old man, ignoring the fact that Mr. Harrison had said sourly that he did not want visitors. But he was determined to further his acquaintance with Gloria.

Charlie Carter knew in his bones that Hamish wanted rid of him. He could not bear the idea of leaving Lochdubh. He was trying to make a cup of tea without breaking or spilling anything when there was a knock at the door. When he opened it, he found Priscilla Halburton-Smythe smiling at him.

"I'm afraid Hamish is out," said Charlie. "I'm about to make tea. Like some?"

"Yes, please." Priscilla sat down at the kitchen table. Various pieces of china, recently mended, stood on a piece of newspaper.

"Have you been breaking much?" she asked sympathetically.

"Hamish gets so mad at me," said Charlie. "And that makes me worse. Fact is, it is a wee station and we're two big men." He poured tea carefully and then sat down gingerly opposite her. Even sitting down, his head was near the low ceiling. The kitchen chair creaked alarmingly under his weight. His normally pleasant face looked so miserable that Priscilla was touched. Because of her beauty, until Charlie came along, Priscilla had never been able to have a male friend.

"I've just remembered something," she said. "In the basement at the castle, there's a little apartment which used to be the butler's place before we turned it into a hotel. It has high ceilings."

Charlie brightened and then his face fell. "I'm supposed to live in police accommodation."

"Nobody would know, apart from me and Hamish. Oh, maybe the villagers, but they won't talk. Let's go now and have a look."

Hamish, as he followed Gloria into the dark hall of the hunting lodge, remembered again that Mr. Harrison was a nasty old man who had sneered at him when Hamish had visited. He carried the shopping basket into a cavernous kitchen. "Just put the basket on the table," said Gloria, "and come through to the drawing room and say hullo."

"Isn't there a housekeeper to do the shopping?" asked Hamish.

"Yes, but this stuff is for me. Mr. Harrison has a Latvian couple to look after him, Juris and Inga Janson. I prefer to cook my own food. Must look after my figure."

Oh, let *me* look after it for you, thought Hamish dreamily.

"Come along," she said briskly.

As he followed her through a dark stone-flagged passage and across the shadowy hall where only weak light filtered through the mullioned windows, Hamish reflected that the hunting box had probably been built at the end of the nineteenth century when there was a craze for Gothic architecture. Stuffed animals' heads looked down from the thick stone walls. A stone staircase with a stone banister led upwards.

Gloria pushed open a heavy oak door, stood aside, and called, "Here is our local bobby to see you, Mr. Harrison."

An old man with his knees covered in a tartan rug was seated in a wheelchair by a French window overlooking a terrace where a few dead leaves skittered along in the breeze.

He swung his chair round. "He's already said hullo. Where the hell are the Jansons? I want a drink."

"I'll get it," said Gloria. "Your usual whisky and soda? What about you, Hamish?"

"Too early for me," said Hamish.

"Sanctimonious prick," commented Mr. Harrison.

He had a thick head of hair and bushy eyebrows. His eyes were small and black.

"You see this copper here, Gloria?" he demanded. "This is just the sort of chap you want to avoid. If he had any guts or ambition, he would have risen in the ranks instead of being stuck in the back of nowhere."

"Like you," said Hamish.

"Here's your drink, my dear," said Gloria

soothingly. "Aren't we a bit cross this morning?"

Mr. Harrison took the glass from her and his face softened. "What would I do without you? Push off, copper."

Hamish smiled. "If you ever need my help, forget it."

"I'll see you out," said Gloria.

Hamish hesitated at the front door. "Any chance of taking you out for dinner one evening? There's a very good restaurant in Lochdubh."

"I'm allowed a day off a week. Every Sunday. Maybe that would be nice."

"What about next Sunday? I'll drive so you can have a drink."

"If Mr. Harrison saw you, I don't think he would approve. I'll get Juris to run me there. What time?"

"Say eight o'clock?"

"Fine."

"You're not going to bring those creepy animals with you, are you?"

"No, not at all," said Hamish, her attractions

dimming a little like a faulty lightbulb. "See you there."

He climbed into the police Land Rover. Sonsie was in the passenger seat and Lugs in the back. "You're not creepy, are you?" he said. Sonsie gave a rumbling purr.

At the police station, he was met by local fisherman Archie Maclean, carrying two mackerel. "Make you a nice wee dinner," he said, handing them over. "I saw you chasing after that flirty nurse."

"Why do you call her flirty?"

"Herself gets the Sundays off and aye gangs up tae the bar at the hotel and sits there till some fellow invites her for dinner."

"Surely not!"

"Aye. As sure as I'm standing here. If you're looking for Charlie, he's gone off with Priscilla."

"Why?" demanded Hamish.

"I dinnae ken. Take the fish."

"Thanks, Archie."

Hamish went slowly into the police

station, where he put the fish in the fridge. He was envious of Charlie's easy-going friendship with Priscilla. He wondered sourly whether Charlie was gay. He had shown no sexual interest in any female so far. But then one of his own best friends was Angela Brodie, the doctor's wife, and he could not ever remember lusting after her.

Curiosity overcame him. He told his animals to stay and went back out to his vehicle and sped off to the hotel.

The manager, Mr. Johnson, said they were down in the basement but he didn't know what they were doing. Hamish made his way down.

"This'll just be grand," he heard Charlie saying. "But maybe Hamish won't like it."

The voices were coming from the far end of the basement where a door stood open.

"Hamish won't like what?" he called.

There was a short silence and then Priscilla called, "In here."

Hamish walked in. He found himself in what seemed to have been a small apartment.

"What d'ye think?" cried Charlie. "Priscilla says I could move in here and you'd have more room at the station."

"What is this place?" asked Hamish.

"It used to be a wee apartment for the butler," said Charlie. The Tommel Castle Hotel had once been the Halburton-Smythes' private residence. When Colonel Halburton-Smythe had fallen on hard times, Hamish had persuaded him to turn the place into a hotel.

Hamish looked round. There was a small living room, furnished simply with a dusty gate-leg table and two hard chairs. By the side of the living room was a small kitchen with a tiny Belling cooker on a counter and some cups and plates covered with dust on the draining board beside a sink.

"The bedroom's through here," said Charlie eagerly. "Priscilla says that the butler, old Mr. Sweeney, was a great tall man."

The bedroom held a long single bed covered in an old mattress stuffed with ticking, flanked by two small chests of drawers.

"How do I square it wi' Strathbane?" asked Hamish.

"They don't need to know," said Priscilla.

Hamish suddenly realised that this could mean he would get his station back, all to himself. Perhaps he could even persuade one pretty nurse to join him there. He went off into a rosy dream.

Priscilla looked with some irritation at the tall sergeant with the flaming-red hair.

"Hamish! Wake up!"

"Oh, aye, grand," said Hamish quickly. "But make sure your phone works down here, Charlie. And God forbid we should have any more major crime, but if we do, you'll need to move back to the station."

"A home of my own!" cried Charlie, sitting down on one of the hard chairs, which promptly splintered under his weight. He turned scarlet as he scrambled to his feet. "I'll repair that, Priscilla. I promise."

"Charlie, it was riddled with woodworm. There's plenty of furniture in the basement for you to choose from. I'll get a couple of the maids to help you."

"No," said Charlie firmly. "I'll do it all myself. I just need some cleaning stuff."

There were some cupboards under the sink. Priscilla bent down and looked into them.

"Well! Look at this. Our old butler seems to have nicked some of the best wines. And here's a bottle of vintage champagne. We'll have a glass each to celebrate."

"You mean the butler was a thief?" asked Charlie.

"It's called butler's privilege. He's dead anyway. I've found some glasses. I'll just rinse them out."

Hamish collected three sturdy chairs from an area of the basement outside, crowded with discarded furniture. Priscilla had just opened the bottle and was pouring out three glasses of champagne when Detective Jimmy Anderson walked into the apartment.

"What's this?" he demanded. "I was on my road to see you, Hamish, when I saw your Land Rover in the hotel car park. You know what I feel about drinking on duty. Got any whisky, Priscilla?"

Priscilla went to the cupboard and brought out a bottle of twelve-year-old malt.

"This do?"

Jimmy's blue eyes gleamed in his foxy face. "Pour it out, lassie."

"What brings you?" asked Hamish.

"Strathbane prison, that's what. I'm rounding up manpower. The search starts this afternoon. The number of weapons, drugs, and mobile phones has doubled in Scottish prisons."

"You could have phoned me," said Hamish.

"Och, I wanted a trip out. Blair is in charge and he's shouting and bullying already. We've got mobile phone detection equipment and drug dogs, so the main search will be for weapons." Detective Chief Inspector Blair was the bane of Hamish Macbeth's life, always trying to get him transferred to Strathbane.

"You should be looking for bent screws," said Charlie. "If it's weapons, then the prison officers must be getting paid to sneak them in."

"Hard going," said Jimmy. "They all cover for each other."

His phone rang. He looked gloomily at the dial. "Blair," he said. "We'd best get going. Man, this whisky is heaven." He slipped the bottle in his pocket.

"You can stay," whispered Hamish to Charlie. "I'll get Jimmy to say you couldnae leave the station unmanned. But collect Sonsie and Lugs. I don't want them left alone too long."

As they approached Strathbane, the skies darkened and a smear of drizzle clouded Hamish's windscreen before he switched the wipers on and looked down the long road to where what he thought of as a boil on the Highlands appeared in the distance.

It had once been a thriving fishing port, but the fishing stock had declined and with it any heavy industry, leaving the town a sink of crime and drugs. The prison was a Victorian one, built to the same design as Wormwood Scrubs.

As they drove up to the entrance, the rain had become a torrent and the wind was rising, moaning in the turrets of the old prison. After they had been through security, a wooden-faced prison officer told them to report to the governor's office.

The governor, Bella Ogilvie, was a small, plump woman. Beside her was a tall woman in police inspector's uniform. She had high Slavic cheekbones, cold grey eyes, and a thin mouth.

"Where have you been, Anderson?" she snapped.

"Collecting reinforcements, ma'am," said Jimmy. "You are ...?"

"Fiona Herring. And no cracks about red herrings. I've heard them all. Who's this?"

"Sergeant Hamish Macbeth, ma'am."

"Heard of you. The pair of you get over to C Wing and search all the cells."

"Where is Mr. Blair?" asked Jimmy.

"Mr. Blair is in hospital."

"What happened?"

Her eyes lit up and she suppressed a laugh. "The detective inspector insulted a police dog called Fred. He told the dog it was a mangy, useless-looking cur and tried to kick it. Fred took offence and bit him in the arse. I have been called in from Inverness to take charge. Off with you."

As Hamish followed Jimmy to C Wing, he reflected that when she had nearly laughed, Fiona had suddenly appeared a very attractive woman.

At the end of a long dreary afternoon, they took their finds back to the governor's office: five knives, one replica gun, and a packet of Ecstasy tablets. The governor told them to take their contraband to the conference room.

Laid out on the long table was a depressing selection of drugs, phones, and weapons. The weapons consisted of knives, sharpened toothbrushes, shivs, and five guns.

"I have a list of the names and addresses of all the prison guards," said Inspector Fiona Herring. "I will allocate names to each officer. I want their backgrounds checked thoroughly. What is it, Governor?"

Mrs. Ogilvie looked like a frightened rabbit. "The guards have gone on strike," she wailed.

"Who is in charge of the union?"

"Blythe Cummings."

"I want him here. Now!"

The governor hurried off.

When it came Hamish's turn, Fiona said, "I think you may go back to your station, Sergeant. You have a large area to cover."

Lovely woman, thought Hamish. The first person in authority to realise the extent of my beat. No rings. Wonder if there's a man in her life.

When Hamish returned to his police station, he found Charlie loading up his old station wagon with his belongings. "You'd better come here every day and report for duty," said Hamish. "I'll miss your company in the evenings but not your big feet. You and Priscilla getting along all right?"

"She's great. Just like a sister."

Hamish pushed back his cap and scratched his red hair as he watched Charlie drive off. What man could survey the beauty that was Priscilla and look on her as a sister?

After Charlie had left, Hamish decided to drive to Braikie. His previous constable, Dick

Fraser, had left to buy a bakery shop with a Polish woman called Anka. Anka was glamorous. Hamish had tried several times to get her out on a date but without success. Surely she and tubby Dick could not be romantically involved.

The shop had just closed for the night when he arrived. He noticed a shiny, brand-new BMW parked outside. If it was Dick's, business must be very good indeed.

He rang the bell to the flat over the shop. Anka Bajorak answered the door. My world is beginning to be peopled by beautiful unavailable women, thought Hamish. But maybe Gloria is available. Anka walked ahead of him up the stairs, her auburn hair tied back in a ponytail and her long legs encased in tight jeans, giving one highland police sergeant a stab of lust.

Dick had slimmed down. But with his grey hair and small figure, he certainly did not look like the type of man to capture the affections of such as Anka. He was comfortably ensconced in an armchair by the peat fire.

"It's yourself, Hamish," cried Dick. "Like a dram?"

"Tea will be fine."

"I'll get it," said Anka.

Hamish told Dick about the visit to the prison and then said, "There's a newcomer in the neighbourhood."

"That'll be the wee nurse," said Dick. "Talk o' the place. Say she dresses like a nurse out o' one o' thae *Carry On* movies. They say she's after the auld man's money."

"The things people say!" complained Hamish. "I've met her. She's charming."

"Oh aye? Got a date?"

"Next Sunday."

"Well, she wouldn't be going out wi' you if she was after money," said Dick.

Anka came back with a cup of tea for Hamish and two cakes. "How's business?" asked Hamish.

"Booming," said Anka. "We thought of opening another shop, but we decided to start a business on the Internet. It's called BapsareUs. We send parcels of baps all over Britain."

"I'm not surprised," said Hamish. One of the usual Scottish laments was that it was almost impossible to get a decent bap, those large breakfast rolls. Anka's baps were famous.

"We've had to build a new place to cope with all the baking and take on lots of staff," said Anka. "Several of the big companies have tried to buy us over."

Hamish told them about Charlie moving out. "Won't you be lonely?" asked Dick.

"No, I'm delighted to get my station back. Charlie is great but he's so clumsy, he's a walking disaster."

"I would like to meet him," said Anka. "Bring him with you next time."

"Will do," said Hamish. "I'd better get back."

When Hamish returned to the station, he found a note on the kitchen table from Charlie. "I've taken Sonsie and Lugs up to the castle. They were mooching at the Italian restaurant and we don't want them getting fat. I'll drop them back later."

The wind had risen, moaning around the

police station. Hamish fought off a sudden feeling of loneliness. But then he had a vision of the pretty Gloria, living with him at the police station. Three days to Sunday and then he would see her again.

Chapter Two

Listen! You hear the grating roar
Of pebbles which the waves draw back,
and fling,
At their return, up the high strand,
Begin, and cease, and then begin again,
With the tremulous cadence slow, and bring
The eternal note of sadness in.

—Matthew Arnold

Colonel Halburton-Smythe arrived back at the Tommel Castle Hotel in a bad mood. He and his wife had been visiting Lord and Lady Fortross over near Oban. Unfortunately, their room had been directly above the bedchamber of their hosts and the fireplace chimney acted as a splendid conduit of sound.

So on the first night, as he was getting ready for bed, he heard Lord Fortross's high complaining voice. "Why did you invite that boring little colonel? I can't abide retired military men who insist on keeping their titles. And the man's a damn stereotype."

The colonel had backed away from the fireplace as if before a snake and had told his startled wife to pack up. They were leaving in the morning.

He was an insecure little man, product of an ambitious father who had made his fortune with a chain of popular shoe shops. Using his fortune, his father had sent him to Eton and then on to Sandhurst Military Academy. The colonel had quickly adopted a personality to fit what he fondly believed was required. He worked hard and, with his father's money, entertained lavishly. He rose rapidly up the ranks and married Philomena Halburton, who hailed from an aristocratic family and had joined the name of Smythe to that of Halburton.

His happiest day was when he quit the army and bought the castle and estates, only to go nearly bankrupt after being tricked into bad investments. Hamish Macbeth saved the day with the hotel idea. Because of excellent fishing and shooting and a first-class manager, the hotel quickly prospered.

On his first day back, the colonel noticed a large man going down to the basement, someone he did not know. He went down and saw the man going into the old butler's apartment and followed him in. He blinked and looked around. A small coal fire was burning briskly. Two comfortable armchairs were drawn up beside it. A faded Chinese carpet that he remembered used to be in the morning room, now the hotel bar, covered the floor.

Standing by the fire was a giant of a man with fair hair and child-like blue eyes.

"Who the hell are you?" demanded the colonel.

So Charlie, in his soft lilting voice, explained while the colonel paced up and down.

"She had no right," raged the colonel. "Priscilla should have consulted me first."

"Well, sir," said Charlie. "Miss Priscilla did think it might be a good idea to have a resident polis, protecting the place. But I'll pack up. Maybe a wee dram, sir?"

The colonel suddenly sighed and sat down in one of the armchairs, all bluster gone. The cosy little room reminded him of the days of his childhood, before his father had become so rich and ambitious. They had lived in a neat little bungalow, warm and safe.

"Yes, I will have a dram," he said.

Charlie poured two stiff drinks and then sat down opposite.

"Tell me about yourself," he said. So Charlie talked about his upbringing in South Uist in the Hebrides, his soft voice lulling the colonel into a rare feeling of peace.

The colonel was suddenly overcome with a desire to tell this gentle giant about his humiliation. Charlie listened carefully. When the colonel had finished, Charlie said, "I mind Lord Fortross. I was visiting relatives in Tiree and himself was over for the snipe shooting. Awful pompous git. Nobody liked him. Talk about bores! Man, he was describing himself."

The colonel beamed and stretched his feet out to the fire. "Any more whisky, laddie?"

Hamish heard a knock at the door later that day and found Priscilla on the doorstep. "I came to say goodbye," she said. "I'm off to London tomorrow. Dad has discovered Charlie."

"Oh, my," said Hamish. "Is he out on his ear?"

"It's the oddest thing. He's taken Charlie trout fishing."

"It isnae the season."

"Sea trout. The pair of them are out on the loch."

"Well, I'm blessed. Aren't you surprised?"

"Not really. Charlie is so kind. All sorts of people gravitate to him."

Hamish's hazel eyes narrowed with jealousy. Did Priscilla fancy him? Then he relaxed. If she was interested in Charlie, she would not be leaving for London.

When they had been engaged, she had been so passionless. Had that been his fault?

"You've gone off into a dream, Hamish," said Priscilla.

"Sorry. I was just thinking how nice and quiet it is now."

"Are Dick and Anka an item?"

"No. Business partners. No romance there."

"I wouldn't be too sure."

"C'mon, Priscilla. Don't be daft. Tubby wee grey-haired Dick and the glorious Anka!"

That evening in the bakery, Anka went upstairs to the living room and found Dick dressed in his best suit. "Are you going out somewhere?" she asked. "That's the suit you wear when we've a meeting with the bank manager. And roses and champagne! What's the occasion? Dick, you've gone quite white."

Dick sank to one knee and held up a small jeweller's box. "Will you do me the very great honour of marrying me?" he said.

Anka threw back her head and laughed. Red in the face, Dick got to his feet. "I'm sorry," he said. "I should have known there wasnae any hope."

"Give me the ring, open the champagne, my love. I thought you would never ask."

Charlie went about his duties during the day, visiting the outlying croft houses to make sure everything was all right. In the evenings, he was now expected to take his dinner with the colonel and his wife and then they all retreated to his little flat for a nightcap. Mrs. Halburton-Smythe was delighted with her husband's new friendship. She had never before known him to be so relaxed and so amiable. She would have liked to invite Hamish to join them, but the colonel stubbornly refused to have anything to do with that "lazy, mooching copper." He had snobbery enough to hope that his beautiful daughter might make a good match and he always feared she might have the folly to become engaged to Hamish again.

On Sunday, Hamish brushed his red hair until it shone, put on his best suit, and made his way to the restaurant. He had reserved a table by the window. The evening was still and the first frost had arrived. The waiter, Willie Lamont, who was once his constable before he married the restaurant owner's daughter, approached with the menu.

"Two menus," said Hamish. "I'm expecting company."

"And who would that be?"

"Mind your own business."

Willie went off and came back with another menu. "What's special tonight?" asked Hamish.

"Something sounds like awfy bokey."

"Probably osso buco," said Hamish, who was used to Willie's malapropisms.

Hamish waited and waited. At last, he found Mr. Harrison's number and phoned. An Eastern European voice answered—the Latvian, Hamish guessed.

"May I speak to Miss Dainty?" he asked. "This is Hamish Macbeth. She was supposed to meet me for dinner this evening."

"Mr. Harrison said she went for a walk. Hasn't come back."

Probably forgot, thought Hamish dismally, after he had rung off. He ordered the osso buco but picked at it, finally gave up, paid the bill, and went back to the station.

"For the first time in my life," he said to his animals, "I could do wi' a nice wee crime to take my mind off things."

Two days went by while Hamish stubbornly stopped himself from phoning the hunting lodge to find out why Gloria had stood him up. It was a fine autumn day. The rowan trees planted at some of the cottage gates to keep the fairies away were bowed down with scarlet berries. The lower slopes of the two tall mountains behind the village were purple with heather.

He took a stroll along the waterfront. He saw the Currie sisters, Nessie and Jessie, approaching and looked wildly round for some means of escape, but they had seen him, so he waited reluctantly until they came up to him. They were unmarried twins and looked remarkably alike with tightly permed grey hair, thick glasses, and identical camel-hair coats.

"I'm glad to see Mr. Harrison's got himself a proper nurse," said Nessie, "and not some wee flibbertigibbet."

"Flibbertigibbet," echoed the Greek chorus that was her sister.

"You mean Gloria Dainty has left?" exclaimed Hamish.

"Went off wi' her suitcase," said Nessie. "Never even left a note."

"When was this?"

"Sunday evening."

Hamish felt a sharp pang of unease. He touched his cap to them and moved on. Suddenly he decided to go out to the hunting lodge.

Juris, the Latvian, answered the door. He was a tall, powerful man. Hamish asked to see Mr. Harrison but was told the old man was lying down and did not want to be disturbed.

"Why did Miss Dainty leave?" asked Hamish. "You were supposed to run her to Lochdubh to have dinner with me on Sunday evening."

"I went to fetch her but she was not there

and all her belongings had gone," said Juris. "On Monday, Mr. Harrison got a new nurse up from an agency in Inverness."

"Didn't she leave a note?"

"No, nothing."

"But when I phoned, you said she'd gone for a walk."

"That's what Mr. Harrison told me. The next day, my wife looked in her room and saw all her things were gone and told him, and he said, 'Good riddance.'"

"Was Miss Dainty involved with a man?"

"If she was, she didn't talk about it."

Hamish could not get any further. He went back to the police station and rang around all the local taxi companies, but Gloria had not called for a taxi. So it followed that someone must have been waiting for her at the end of the drive.

Well, she had gone, and that was that.

A day later, a burglary was reported at an ironmonger's in Braikie. Hamish called Charlie, picked him up at the hotel, and sped off. The owner, a tall highlander called Josh Andrews, pointed to the door. "It looks as if they opened it with a crowbar," he said.

"What was taken?" asked Hamish.

"I have a list right here."

Hamish looked down a long list of expensive power tools. "I'd better get the forensic boys over," he said. "We'll need to look for fingerprints. Have you contacted the insurance company?"

"Not yet."

"They'll want to send an investigator."

"What for?" demanded Josh angrily. "You see the door's been jemmied. You've got the list. Chust put in your report, laddie."

"It is like this," said Hamish gently. "Shopkeepers often stage a burglary when they fall on hard times. And their investigators are like ferrets. They'll search and search to make sure you're not pulling a fast one. I 'member some poor soul ower in Cnothan. Faked a burglary and got a criminal record."

"Are you calling me a liar?"

"Waud I dae a cruel thing like that," said Hamish, his accent strengthening. "I'll chust be having a wee keek out back."

"What for?"

"They could have escaped that way. I gather it took place at night?"

"Must have done."

"So they would not want to be seen loading stuff out on the main street. Stand aside."

"No, you need a warrant."

"Don't be daft," said Charlie. He moved forward and picked up the large man as if he weighed nothing at all and set him to one side.

"*No!*" shouted Josh, and a tear rolled down one cheek.

Hamish looked at Charlie. "Do you see any signs of a break-in?"

"Cannae say I do, sir."

Hamish handed Josh back his list. "Listen to me. I cannot be bothered charging you. I know times are hard. Put a big sign in your window saying 'Autumn Sale. Everything Must Go. Everything Reduced.' Then you knock a couple of quid off the items you said were stolen, along with everything else. Folk love to think they're getting a bargain."

"I'm sorry," said Josh brokenly.

"Oh, get off your sorry arse and get to work," said Hamish. "Come along, Charlie."

"It's a shame," said Charlie as they climbed into the Land Rover.

"Never mind," said Hamish. "There's a grand wee café up the coast on the road to Kinlochbervie. We'll have a cup of coffee and a bun. It's a grand day."

The café was called Westering Home. There were two tables outside facing a long curve of white sandy beach. Hamish and Charlie contentedly drank coffee and munched currant buns until Hamish reluctantly said they had better be getting back.

They were driving along the one-track road beside the beach where two boys were playing when Hamish suddenly flung on the brakes and screeched to a halt. Lugs, in the back, let out a startled yelp.

"What's up?" asked Charlie.

But Hamish was out and running towards the boys.

"Where did you get that?" he demanded.

A small tousle-haired child held up a dripping wet nurse's cap. "It just floated in," he said. "We wasnae doing anything wrong."

Charlie had followed Hamish. "What's up?"

"Unless I am mistaken, that's thon missing nurse's cap," said Hamish, taking a forensic bag out of his pocket and sliding the cap in. "Let's search around a bit before we call Strathbane."

"Strong currents here, I've heard," said Charlie. "If she's in the sea, she could be halfway to America. Here, you boys. Names and addresses and I'll call on your parents later."

When the boys had scampered off, Hamish said, "I'll take the west end of the beach and you try the east."

Hamish made his way to where the cliffs rose up against the pale-blue sky. Seagulls wheeled and dived. All the while, his mind worked busily. She surely wouldn't have left wearing her nurse's uniform. At the foot of the cliffs were jagged needle rocks like pointing fingers. As he approached, two things struck him. That old familiar smell of death and the buzzing of flies.

With a beating heart, he picked his way

among the rocks. Between two of the pointing rocks lay the shattered body of Gloria Dainty under a heaving canopy of black flies.

After Charlie had joined him, they put police tape round the rocks. "I think she was thrown over," said Hamish. "Go up to the top of the cliffs and cordon off an area there as well. I've phoned it in. You're a bit white, Charlie. You've got the boys' addresses, haven't you?"

"Aye, they're in Kinlochbervie."

"Get ower there and take a statement, and then knock on some doors and see if anyone saw or heard anything. Take the Land Rover. When you've finished, let Sonsie and Lugs out for a run and then come back here."

Hamish waited, sitting on a flat rock, hoping that the bane of his life Detective Chief Inspector Blair would decide not to come. He wanted to go back to the body, brush the flies away, and find out if she had been dead before she was thrown over. But he knew he would be accused of contaminating the crime scene. Flies, not yet maggots. If she had been killed elsewhere and then dumped, that would account for the flies. Had the seagulls been at the body? They ate carrion, that he knew.

It was an hour before he heard the sound of the whole contingent from Strathbane arriving outside the café and stood up. With relief, he saw it was his friend Detective Jimmy Anderson heading the group. His foxy face looked as hung over as usual.

"What have we got, Hamish?" he asked.

"A private nurse to old Mr. Harrison. I had a date wi' her on the Sunday. She didnae show and I thought I had been stood up. Mr. Harrison said she had gone for a walk. The Latvian who works for him said her belongings were gone. I had finished investigating a false alarm in Braikie and came up here because it's on my beat. Two laddies, playing on the shore, had a nurse's cap and I recognised it as being the type that Gloria had worn. I searched and found her behind those rocks. I think she was thrown over. Lots of flies. But she disappeared four days ago."

"Here's the pathologist, Hamish. Let's go to thon café and leave him to work."

Jimmy found to his delight that the café sold liquor and bought a half bottle of whisky and poured a slug into his coffee.

"So where's Blair?" asked Hamish.

"Sulking. He wanted a transfer to Glasgow, but they didnae want him."

"But he would be daft to get away from the protection of Superintendent Daviot!"

"Aye. But he doesnae know that. Thinks he's the best detective since Sherlock Holmes."

"Who was fictional," said Hamish.

"Well, our Blair is a legend in his own lunchtime. It only takes a few drams to make him think he is Sherlock Holmes. So when was your date wi' the nurse?"

"Sunday. Pretty lassie. It's a damn shame. Mind you, I heard our Gloria liked to go to the Tommel Castle Hotel on her day off and pick up men in the bar."

"Would old Harrison have killed her?"

"He's confined to a wheelchair."

"What about this Latvian?"

"Don't know much about him. He and his wife work for Harrison. The body's covered in flies. Doesn't it take about three days afore they turn into maggots?"

"Something like that."

"Or maybe she was killed elsewhere and then the dead body thrown over. Oh, here's Charlie. Found anything?"

"Nothing," said Charlie.

"I'm waiting for the pathologist's report," said Hamish, "and then we'll maybe look at the top of the cliffs, but it's no use looking up there if it turns out she wasn't thrown over."

Charlie pulled up a chair and sat down. The incoming waves, green near the shore and aquamarine further out, curled and splashed on the beach while restless seagulls swooped and dived.

At last, Hamish could see the pathologist emerging from the rocks. He was a man new to Hamish, tall and shambling with a long grey beard. He joined them at the table as an ambulance lurched down onto the beach.

"I'll know better when I get a full autopsy," he said. "I would estimate she's been dead about four days, but possibly dumped over the cliff maybe yesterday. The flies are pretty fresh. She's been strangled but she's got a lot of broken bones showing that she was tossed from the cliffs."

"Come on, Charlie," said Hamish. "We'd best get up there."

"I'll get over to Harrison's," said Jimmy. "Oh, oh! Here comes trouble."

Police Inspector Fiona Herring came striding up to them. The pathologist made his escape. "This is a cosy tea party," she said.

"What are you doing here?" demanded Jimmy.

"I have been drafted in to gee up what I am told is a slack lot," she said. "Fill me in."

Jimmy told her what he knew. Hamish described his failed date.

"I'm off to interrogate Harrison," said Jimmy, "and Hamish and Charlie are going to search the top of the cliffs."

"I've a squad of men who can do that," she said. "Carter can join them. You can supervise, Anderson. I'll take Macbeth to Harrison's. He knows the man."

"May I remind you, ma'am, that I am in charge of this case," said Jimmy furiously.

"Not now. Superintendent Daviot's orders. Come along, Macbeth."

"May I point out that Macbeth was trying to date her?" said Jimmy. "That makes him a suspect."

"Dear me. A friend in need is a pain in the arse," said Fiona, flicking a contemptuous look at Jimmy. "She disappeared on Sunday evening. Where were you, Macbeth?"

"Sitting in the Italian restaurant in Lochdubh, waiting for her until ten o'clock, ma'am. Then I went back to the station. I phoned my mother in Rogart for a wee chat and then I went to bed."

"Sounds all right to me. Come along. We'll take my car."

Hamish gave directions to her driver, fighting down a feeling of hurt that Jimmy had tried to suggest he was a suspect.

"So you tried to date the girl," said Fiona. "I gather she was attractive when not thrown down a cliff and covered with flies."

"She was very pretty," said Hamish sadly. "Dainty, like her name. I didn't know about her picking up men at the hotel although that might just be village gossip. I'll check later."

"Hope it is village gossip," said Fiona, "or it widens the field." She took out her phone and called Jimmy, instructing him to get over to the Tommel Castle Hotel and make sure none of the guests was allowed to leave until they had been interrogated.

"Why do they call these places 'boxes'?" she asked.

"Well, it meant you had a grand mansion somewhere and this was just a place for the hunting, shooting, and fishing. But I call to mind, it was originally the residence of a snob-bish family in Victorian times who wanted folk to think they were landed gentry. He manufac-tured drainpipes. They called it their hunting box but they didn't really have anywhere else. He had it built after he retired."

"And what is Mr. Harrison's story?"

"Now, there's a thing, ma'am. Usually I find out everything about a newcomer on my beat, but he was so obnoxious, my curiosity died. He's got a Latvian couple working for him. The man, Juris, speaks good English so I don't think they're new immigrants. But it's Mr. Harrison who bothers me. He doted on Gloria and yet his final comment was 'Good riddance.'"

"What about heirs?" asked Fiona. "I mean, if it got on the family grapevine that he was sweet on his nurse, someone might have seen their inheritance at risk."

Her mobile phone rang. "Yes, Blair," Hamish heard her say. He listened as outraged squawks came from the other end of the phone. Then Fiona said in a voice as cold as ice, "If you have any complaint about me being in charge of the case, take it up with your superiors. Furthermore, as there is no proof that the Latvian had anything to do with it, I would be careful about airing your prejudices against immigrants. If I may put it politely, sod off!"

What an amazon, thought Hamish gleefully.

The early dark of a highland autumn lay over the countryside as they drove up the drive to the hunting box. "Has this place got a name?" asked Fiona.

"It's always been called Dunlop's Folly. Dunlop was the original owner."

The black Gothic turreted building stood up against the starry sky. The police driver stopped the car outside the huge brass-studded front door.

"Now," said Fiona. "Let's see what we can see."

Chapter Three

These are much deeper waters than I had thought.
—Sir Arthur Conan Doyle

Juris answered the door and surveyed them doubtfully. "I don't know if the boss is up to seeing you," he said.

"We will start with you," said Fiona briskly. "Is there some room we can use for interviewing? And we will need to talk to your wife."

"Maybe the library," said Juris. "It is never used."

They walked across the shadowy hall under the glassy eyes of the stuffed animals, shining in the dim illumination of several wall lights.

Juris pushed open a door and ushered them
in after switching on the overhead light. The
original owner had belonged to the class who
bought their books by the yard. Great dreary
calf-bound tomes lined the walls from floor to
ceiling. There was a large desk against the window in front of dusty velvet curtains. Fiona sat
behind the desk and indicated that Juris should
sit in front of her. Hamish leaned against a
wall and surveyed the man. Juris was tall and
powerful, with a thick head of hair over a low
forehead, marked by strong bushy eyebrows.

Fiona took out a small tape recorder and laid
it on the desk.

Before she could begin, Hamish said, "You
are a British citizen, aren't you?"

"Yes, and the wife as well."

"So why do they call you Latvian?" asked
Fiona.

"Our parents on both sides were Latvian.
There is a Latvian community in Glasgow. Up
here, if you're from Glasgow, you're a foreigner.
Folk asked why we had such odd names. Told
them. Called the Latvians ever since."

"When did you start work for Mr. Harrison?"

"Last February. He hired us from an agency in Glasgow." Juris's voice held only a trace of a Glaswegian accent.

"And where were you before that?"

"Worked for Lord Kinbochy in Gourock."

"Why did you leave?"

"He died and his place was being sold up by the heirs. Mr. Harrison offered good pay. My wife is a grand cook."

"Right. Now to the night Gloria Dainty disappeared. Her body has just been found at the bottom of cliffs near Kinlochbervie."

Juris bowed his head in silence. The highland grapevine is marvellous, thought Hamish. Probably the whole of Sutherland knew Gloria was dead.

"So take your time. What happened on the night she disappeared?"

"She had a date with Hamish Macbeth. When he phoned, I asked Mr. Harrison and he said she had gone out for a walk. But when my wife looked in her room the next day, all her belongings were gone. I told Mr. Harrison. He was furious. He said, 'Good riddance,' but I think he was hurt because he was sweet on her."

"An old disabled man?"

"She flirted with him something awful. My wife said she was hoping to be left money in his will, but I think she hoped to get him to marry her."

"What makes you think that?"

"I came in one day and she was sitting on his lap with her arms around his neck and saying, 'Don't you ever want a wife?'"

Fiona opened her capacious handbag and took out a notepad. "Go away and write down all your movements for the evening she disappeared and the following day. I need your age and if you have any other address. But first send your wife in."

When he was gone, Fiona asked Hamish, "What do you think?"

"I think he's decent."

"Your famous highland intuition tells you that?"

"Maybe. It wasnae working verra well when

it came to Gloria. But och, she dressed like a fantasy nurse." Hamish blushed.

The door opened and Inga Janson came in. Fiona asked her all the questions she had asked her husband.

Then Hamish said, "Tell me, Mrs. Janson. What did you think of Gloria Dainty?"

"Wee hoor," she said viciously. "Couldn't leave anything in trousers alone. But the boss didn't know that. 'Ooh, I do like a mature man, Mr. Harrison, dear.'" Inga's voice had risen to a falsetto. She was a plain-faced woman with her hair screwed tightly back into a bun. "She even made a pass at my Juris," said Inga. "'I'll slit your throat if you try any more of that,' and so I told her." Inga gave an exclamation of dismay and covered her mouth with her hand.

"Did you murder her?" asked Fiona bluntly.

"No, I did not!" protested Inga. "I wish she'd never come here. Juris told me about her being murdered. I was glad. But I had nothing to do with it."

Fiona gave her another notebook to write down all her movements. Before she left, Fiona said, "Tell Mr. Harrison we need to search the house. I can get a warrant but it would be easier if he would cooperate."

Inga left and returned after ten minutes to say the search could go ahead. Fiona phoned and demanded a forensic team.

"Now, Macbeth," she said, "if Harrison won't come to see us, we'd better go and see him."

"I'll lead the way," said Hamish. "I think I know where he'll be. If Gloria was picking up men at the hotel, that does widen the field of suspects."

But there was someone who was the last person that Hamish Macbeth would ever consider as a suspect.

Charlie had been dismissed by Jimmy Anderson. Jimmy was enjoying looking as if he were in charge. He had addressed the press, who had gathered like gannets. He knew he would be on the evening news. He didn't want Charlie around because Hamish Macbeth had a nasty way of solving cases and he didn't want his sidekick reporting anything to him.

When he descended to the hotel basement, Charlie was startled to find a white-faced and nervous Colonel Halburton-Smythe waiting for him. "You've got to help me!" cried the colonel.

"I'll do what I can, sir," said Charlie. "What's up? Poachers?"

"If that were all. We're friends, right? Call me George."

"Well...er...George," said Charlie soothingly, "let's have a wee dram. I'll put some more peat on the fire. We'll get comfy."

Once the fire was blazing and the colonel had knocked back a shot of whisky, Charlie said, "Let's be having it."

"I hear that nurse has been found murdered," said the colonel.

"Yes, sad business."

"I'm a suspect," said the colonel miserably.

"You! No, that cannae be right."

"It was like this," said the colonel heavily. "My manager, Mr. Johnson, said he was feeling uneasy about her, that she was picking up men in the bar. He told me her name. I said I'd deal with it. There she was, with two of the male guests. She was wearing a very low-cut black dress and high heels. I'd got her name, so I said, 'Step outside, Miss Dainty. I would like a word with you.'

"I took her into the office and sent the manager away. I told her about our concerns and she began to cry. She sobbed that she was lonely and only came up to the hotel for a bit of company. She threw herself into my arms. I felt like a beast. My wife was away. I soothed her down and said we would have a bit of dinner and talk about it.

"I can't remember any woman ever flirting with me before. I was in raptures. She told me a sad story about being stuck out in the wilds with old Harrison and on very little pay. I was so sorry for her. I told her to wait a minute. I had bought my wife an expensive cashmere sweater. I got it and presented it to her, and she kissed me! On the mouth! And in front of the waiters."

"When was this?" asked Charlie.

"It would be the Sunday before she disap-

peared. Two days later, I went over to con-
front old Harrison and I demanded to know
why he was paying her so little. He told me
what she was earning and it was a lot. She was
out. I left a message to say she was not welcome at the hotel again. I felt an old fool who
had been conned. Now the staff at the hotel will be questioned and my dinner with her
will all come out."

"That sweater, was it wrapped up?" asked
Charlie.

"No, I hadn't wrapped it yet."

"So she left it in the office and you went to
get it for her. Now, as long as Detective Chief
Inspector Blair keeps off the case, it won't be
too bad. We'll work out a statement down at
the station and make it look oh so innocent. I'll
type it up."

"What if Macbeth tells my daughter?"

"You don't know him very well. As far as we
are concerned, the little tart threw herself at
you. Come along, sir—I mean, George—and
we'll get it over with."

Hamish was not at the station. Charlie typed

up the statement and left it in the office after the colonel had signed it.

They had just returned to the hotel when Charlie got a call from Hamish to say the inspector was driving him to the station and Charlie had better be there.

Hamish Macbeth reflected sourly that he would never, ever understand women. Seated in the station kitchen, the normally hard-bitten Fiona had taken one look at Charlie and her face had softened. She had questioned him about his life, his ambitions, and whether he had a girlfriend. A transformed Charlie had glowed under all the attention.

There was Anka as well, thought Hamish, who refused all his invitations unless they included Dick.

Fiona read Charlie's report on the colonel and Charlie said, "He is an innocent, ma'am, and a great friend o' mine. He's frightened he'll be suspected of the murder."

"I think that is highly unlikely," said Fiona. "I see from the first reports sent in from the hotel that the Sunday Gloria disappeared, the colonel and his lady were over in Caithness at Lord Clardey's shooting party. They left on the Friday and did not get back to the hotel until the Monday, so what's the silly man worried about?"

"When there's a murder, ma'am," said Charlie sententiously, "everyone feels guilty."

"You are a very wise young man," Fiona said, while Hamish felt like howling, *What in the name o' the wee man is so damn clever about that?*

Fiona looked around. "You are two very big men and this is a small station. How do you both fit in?"

"We manage, ma'am," said Charlie quickly.

"I see the statement from Colonel Halburton-Smythe was made to you, Charlie."

Oh, first names, is it? thought Hamish.

"I'll go up to the hotel and put his fears at rest," continued Fiona. "You come with me, Charlie. Macbeth, tomorrow, get back up to those cliffs. You have a reputation for finding out what everyone else misses."

"How did you get on with Mr. Harrison?" asked Charlie.

"He'd got himself a new slab-faced nurse who protects him like a rottweiler. When we approached him, his eyes were closed and the nurse, a Helen Mackenzie, said he had just had one of his turns and to please leave. I was about to insist that we wait until he felt better when she said if Mr. Harrison died because of our harassing him, his son would sue our socks off. He'd already been on to Daviot, so I got a phone call from the super to order me out of there."

"The lawyer didn't block the search team, surely," said Charlie.

"No, that went ahead. Couldn't find a thing."

When they had left, Lugs stared up at his master with his odd blue eyes.

"I hope she disnae find out Charlie's living at the hotel," said Hamish. "Oh, to hell with it. Come on. I'm going to the Italian restaurant. I could do wi' comfort food."

Charlie had failed to tell the colonel that his bosses did not know he was living at the hotel. The colonel greeted Charlie warmly and Fiona nervously. "Is there somewhere we can sit?" asked Fiona as they stood in the entrance hall.

And to Charlie's horror, he heard the colonel say, "We can use Charlie's place. I lit the fire."

Fiona said nothing until they were in the little apartment and Charlie had arranged chairs for the three of them in front of the fire.

"Peat fires are supposed to send out a pleasant scent," said Fiona, "but I always think they smell like old socks. Right, Colonel. According to Charlie here, you are worried about your dinner with the dead woman. But you have a cast-iron alibi."

"Gloria kissed me in front of the staff," mumbled the colonel, staring at the worn hearthrug.

"The dead woman had a reputation of being a shameless flirt at best and a nymphomaniac and gold digger at the worst. I am not here to interrogate you. I am here to ask you to go upstairs and gather the staff, such as are not on duty, in the reception. I want to ask them questions."

"Certainly." The colonel beamed at Charlie. "Follow me up. I think your best bet is the maids. They have rooms at the top. I would start with them first. The waiters will be serving dinner."

The most forthcoming maid was, to Fiona's relief, Scottish, and prepared to talk freely, unlike the other three who hailed from Eastern Europe. Her name was Elsie Dunbar, a small girl with a mop of black hair and a spotty face.

"I can tell you about one man," she said. "It was Mr. Fitzwilliam. He's left now. I went to clean the room because he was due to leave and it was past the checkout time. I heard an angry voice and a woman shouting."

"And you listened at the door?" prompted Charlie.

She blushed. "Oh, well, I was that curious. I heard a woman shouting, 'I don't do this sort of thing for nothing.' Then I heard the man say nastily, 'Get out, you slut.' She came out crying and nearly knocked me over."

Fiona turned to the manager, who was listening. "We'll need Fitzwilliam's address and phone number. Anyone else, Miss Dunbar?"

"That's all I know. The other maids don't talk much to me, them being foreign."

When she left, Charlie suggested, "What about the barman? That's where she was supposed to pick men up."

The barman supplied six names of guests, but they all had left. Mr. Johnson, the manager, went off to check the records for addresses.

"I think that's enough for now, and I'm hungry," said Fiona.

"Charlie usually joins us for dinner," said the colonel. "I would be honoured if you would be my guest."

Fiona flashed an amused look at Charlie and said, "Lead the way. Most kind of you."

The colonel saw to his alarm that his wife was already seated at their usual table. But Fiona began to question Charlie about what he thought about the case so far. Charlie shrugged his broad shoulders. "The suspects seem to be building up," he said. "It's going to take a lot of research unless Hamish gets one of his flashes of intuition."

"He seems to have a great track record," said Fiona.

"Overrated," said the colonel crossly.

"Now, dear," his wife put in, "you are only cross because he broke off his engagement with Priscilla. Priscilla is our daughter, Inspector."

"I was delighted," said the colonel. "My only fear is that they might get back together again. I just wish Priscilla would find someone decent, like Charlie here."

"I am sure all the local ladies are after Charlie." Fiona looked amused.

"I havenae noticed," protested Charlie.

Mrs. Halburton-Smythe began to talk about a fund-raiser to start a food bank in Braikie for the poor.

"The trouble about those food banks," said Fiona, "is that the elderly who really need help are too proud to go and it is too often the layabouts who want to keep money for what they consider essentials like cigarettes and booze."

"Maybe not all," said Charlie gently. "I'll help out on my day off, if you like."

The colonel and his wife beamed at Charlie.

They look on him almost like a son, thought Fiona.

After a comforting dinner, Hamish strolled back to the station with his pets at his heels. Once inside, he phoned Mr. Johnson at the hotel and received the news that both Fiona and Charlie were dining with the colonel and his wife. He was in the office when he heard the kitchen door opening and then Jimmy Anderson's voice calling, "Anyone at home?"

Hamish went through to the kitchen. Jimmy looked tired but sober.

"What a day. I could do wi' a dram."

"Oh, all right. But just the one."

Jimmy sat down at the kitchen table. "Where's Old Iron Knickers?"

"Herself is up at the castle, dining with Charlie and the colonel and his missus."

"Charlie! But he's only a constable. What about me? Or at least, you."

"She likes Charlie. I often wonder about our Charlie. Women fancy him but he doesnae even bat a hormone."

Jimmy took a gulp of whisky. "Probably a virgin."

"In this wicked day and age?"

"Could be. Doesnae fancy you, does he?"

"Not a bit. I've got to search the area up there again. Find anything?"

"The pathologist said that the tide didn't reach where she was and maybe she was killed elsewhere and dumped."

"Was she strangled with hands or a ligature?"

"He thinks it could ha' been done wi' something like a scarf."

"No sign of her luggage?" asked Hamish.

Jimmy sighed. "Probably at the bottom of a peat bog somewhere."

"You'd better stay the night," said Hamish. "I'll put clean sheets in the cell."

"The mattress in that cell is as hard as buggery. Anyway, how do you know a storm is coming? Heard it on the radio?"

"Heard it in my bones."

"Don't believe you. I'm off. It's Hallowe'en on Saturday. Expect any trouble?"

"Nothing up here," said Hamish. "Usually just wee kids out guising."

Jimmy left by the kitchen door. The station was protected by the tall cliffs at the end of the sea loch. It was only when he was driving along the waterfront that he became aware of the force of the wind. As he moved up onto the moors, the wind shrieked and buffeted at the car. He had just gained the top of a hill when an enormous blast hit the car and blew it over on its side. Jimmy was pinned by the air bag. His car lights were still working, and he saw to his horror that the first flurries of snow were dancing in their beams.

Jimmy felt like crying. He couldn't reach his pocket to get out his mobile phone.

Then his car was lit up by an approaching vehicle. It stopped behind him. The next thing he knew Hamish Macbeth appeared on the passenger side, wrenched open the door, leaned over and stuck a knife in the air bag, and slowly and carefully hauled Jimmy out.

"Thanks," said Jimmy. "I thought I was a goner. Miracle you turned up."

"No miracle," said Hamish, helping him into the Land Rover. "I realised that wee car of yours might run into trouble. Anything broken?"

"Don't think so."

"I'll get the local garage to rescue your car in the morning. Let's get out o' here. It's going to get worse."

The world had turned into a blinding white wilderness. Hamish drove through it, leaning forward to make sure he did not go off the road.

Jimmy gave a gasp of relief as he was once more back in the sanctuary of the station.

"I could do with a dram as well," said Hamish. "What a night!"

"No point in you searching for clues tomorrow," said Jimmy, seizing the whisky bottle and pouring out a couple of stiff drams. ✓

"It'll be melted by then," said Hamish. "Listen! The gale's moved round to the west."

"How the hell you opt to live in this scary part o' the world is beyond me," said Jimmy.

"According to the Herring woman," said Hamish, "Harrison got a lawyer, had a faint fit, and they couldnae talk to him. Didnae they

point out that you cannae get a lawyer in Scotland unless the police let you have one?"

"I think that applies after you've been
charged. Tell you what," said Jimmy. "Let's have
a crack at the auld scunner ourselves. That'd be
one in the eye for Iron Knickers."

As they set out the next morning, Jimmy was
amazed to see the snow had melted and only a
light breeze danced over the glittering waves on
the loch.

"How disabled is old Harrison?" asked
Jimmy. "When folk start calling lawyers, it's
usually a sign they're as guilty as hell."

"I thought of that," said Hamish. "I'd like a
keek at his medical records. Have you thought
of sending a search team to look over the hotel?"

"That would be stepping on Herring's toes.
Anyway, there wouldnae be any traces of blood.
She was strangled."

"I was thinking that there might have been
some sort of a struggle. Furniture kicked. That
sort of thing."

"I'll put it to her." Jimmy phoned the hotel to find that Fiona and Charlie had left to go to Strathbane to study any reports on the guests that might already have come in. He phoned Fiona at police headquarters and told her *his* idea.

"Your idea, Jimmy?"

"Och, Hamish, I need all the kudos I can get. You don't want promotion. I want Blair's job. He cannae go on knocking back the booze forever."

Hamish drove up the drive towards the hunting box. "Michty me!" exclaimed Jimmy. "When folk say box you expect a square building. Now I see it in daylight, it looks as if it belongs to the Addams family."

Juris answered the door. To Jimmy's request, he shrugged and said, "I'll try."

They waited in the gloom of the hall. "This place is so creepy," said Jimmy, "wi' all those stags heads on the wall that you expect to see something awful up there, like a human head."

Juris came back. "He will see you," he said. "Come this way."

He led them into the room where Gloria had taken Hamish. Mr. Harrison was in his motorised wheelchair, covered in a tartan rug. Behind him as if on guard stood his new nurse, Helen Mackenzie. She was wearing a uniform consisting of a dark-blue dress with a white collar, thick stockings, and clumpy black shoes. She had thick grey hair under a plain white cap. She had small, very green eyes under heavy brows and a nose that any Roman emperor would have been proud of. Hamish never damned any woman as being plain or ugly be-cause he knew that often they had charming characters. But Helen opened her mouth and said in a harsh, bullying voice, "Five minutes. That's all."

"May we sit down?" asked Jimmy.

"You won't be here long enough for that," said Helen, folding muscular arms across her flat chest.

"Get them chairs, for God's sake," growled Mr. Harrison.

Jimmy waited until he and Hamish were seated opposite Mr. Harrison. "How did you come to be crippled?" asked Hamish before Jimmy could speak.

"Five years. Came off my horse and broke my back."

"Where did you live before you came up here?" asked Jimmy.

"Outside Ripon in Yorkshire."

Hamish opened his mouth to ask if Mr. Harrison had originally hailed from the East End of London, because under his posh voice were undertones of Cockney, but Jimmy scowled at him as a signal to keep quiet.

"Now, after Miss Dainty disappeared," said Jimmy, "you are reported to have said, 'Good riddance.' Had you had a quarrel?"

"I had an anonymous letter saying that Gloria had been chatting up men at that hotel. I challenged her with it. She said it was all lies. I told her to get lost. When I heard she had gone out, I was still furious, but now I miss her like hell."

"How did she get to the hotel?"

"Juris usually ran her over."

Jimmy turned to the nurse. "Get Juris in here."

When Juris came in, Jimmy said, "According to you, Gloria had gone out for a walk."

"That's what I was told. I had work to do so I left her to it. When my wife found her belongings missing the next day, we thought she'd decided to leave altogether."

Jimmy turned back to Mr. Harrison. "So you employed Miss Mackenzie here."

"Lucky to get her," said Harrison. "At first, no one at that agency in Strathbane wanted to bury themselves up here, but Miss Mackenzie took the job."

"What is the name of the agency?"

"Private Nursing. Juris will get you the address."

"How does one get out of here apart from the front door?" asked Hamish.

Juris said, "There's the kitchen door and beside that, the old tradesman's entrance. Then, often the windows in this room aren't locked because often Mr. Harrison likes to sit out on the terrace."

Jimmy continued the questioning, asking Mr. Harrison for his previous address in Ripon, his age, and full name. "I am seventy-two and my full name is Percival Danby Harrison."

"With your permission, sir, we'd like to take a look around."

"Knock yourself out," said Mr. Harrison.

"Pity he's so crippled," said Jimmy as they started to walk around the outside of the building, "or he might have strangled her in a rage."

"That's a powerful motorised wheelchair," said Hamish. "Let's look in the garages. Might have an invalid car."

Juris followed them and unlocked the door of one of the two garages. "Now, that's a pretty good invalid car," Jimmy said.

"Mr. Harrison doesn't use it," said Juris. "He prefers to be driven. Your team of searchers went over it. Found nothing."

Jimmy's phone rang and Hamish listened patiently as Jimmy said, "Yes, ma'am," and "No, ma'am."

When Jimmy finally rang off, Hamish said, "What was that all about?"

"She says you're to get back to where the

body was found and look around. I'm to go back to headquarters. Checked on Juris's previous employment. Impeccable record."

"What about Gloria's background?"

"Did her training in Glasgow, worked a bit at Strathbane Hospital, but decided to go in for private nursing. Harrison was her second job. Found her sister, Joyce, who's on her road up. Charlie's coming up to join you."

"So Herring has let him loose."

"Seems like that. You'll need to take me back to see if they've got my car in working order."

Apart from needing a new air bag, Jimmy's car was pronounced roadworthy. Charlie was waiting at the station.

"How are you getting on wi' the new boss?" asked Hamish.

"Grand. Blair is furious. All the time we were going through the stuff on the guests, he paced up and down behind us until she complained."

"Blair can be dangerous when crossed," said Hamish. "He's probably planning something

nasty for her. Let's get going. We'll take the animals."

They were driving along the waterfront when
the tweedy figure of Mrs. Wellington, the minister's wife, waved them down.

"What is it?" asked Hamish.

"Your constable has not been to church," she
boomed.

"There's a murder enquiry going on," said
Hamish. "Charlie hasnae had time to go to the
kirk."

"If you do not ask the Good Lord for help,
you will never solve it," said Mrs. Wellington.

"I'll get in touch right away," said Hamish,
letting in the clutch and speeding off.

Outside Kinlochbervie, he parked outside the
café and he and Charlie made their way along
to where the body had been found. "I'm hungry," said Charlie.

"We'll get a bite in a minute," said Hamish.
"Now, if Dick Fraser were here, he'd have the
table and stove out and be cooking up a full
meal. Maybe we had better get up to the top of

the cliffs. If she was thrown over, there would be nothing down here. Oh, hell, let's eat first."

After bacon baps and strong tea and cans of animal food for Lugs and Sonsie, they climbed up to the top of the cliffs. "That storm might have wiped out anything useful," said Charlie. "And the trouble with heather is that any vehicle wouldn't leave tracks."

"Let's walk back towards the road," said Hamish. "I would like to get my hands on her luggage. I don't think those guests, or Harrison or Juris, would know about peat bogs, and there aren't any around here. Say I'm the murderer. Unless I am some sort of serial killer, this is my first. I chuck the dead body over. I've got the cases in the back. What would I do with them?"

"Throw them in the sea," said Charlie.

"Och, this is a waste of time," grumbled Hamish. "It's getting dark."

They made their way back to the Land Rover. "The guisers are out," commented Charlie. "Hallowe'en already."

There were three small boys. "Penny for the guiser," they chanted.

Hamish fished in his pocket. "Fifty pee, and that's your lot. Hey, wait a minute. Where did you get those clothes?"

They were all wearing women's dresses which trailed on the ground, expensive-looking dresses. One was carrying a tattie bogle, a lantern made out of a scooped-out turnip. For hundreds of years in Scotland, it was the tradition to dress up as spirits of the dead until it changed to children wearing disguises and going out guising.

"My mum found them," said one of the boys. "Finders keepers."

"Listen you, laddie," said Hamish. "Those clothes are part o' a murder enquiry. We've got to talk to your mother right away."

Chapter Four

'Tis now the very witching time of night,
When churchyards yawn and hell itself breathes out
Contagion to this world

—Shakespeare

The mother who had found the clothes was at first defiant. Her name was Annie Eskdale. She was a very small woman wearing an old-fashioned wraparound pinafore over a faded T-shirt and tracksuit bottoms. Although in her thirties, discontent had marred her face with early wrinkles. Her eyes were small and radiating suspicion. The council house she lived in was dingy and smelled of cabbage.

At first, she whined that the clothes were her own. Hamish twisted back the neckline of the dress her son was wearing and said, "How could you afford to pay for an Armani dress?"

"Thrift shop," she screeched.

Charlie produced a pair of handcuffs and held them up. "I am charging you with defeating the ends of justice. A right shame it is, too. Social services will look after your boy."

She broke down and, between sobs, said she had found two suitcases up on the moors. She hadn't meant to do wrong, but times were hard. Her man had left her.

Hamish turned to the boys. "Take off those dresses and I'll give you five pounds. Gentle now," he cautioned as they scrambled out of them. "Now, Mrs. Eskdale, where are the cases?"

"Out the back."

They followed her out through a kitchen piled with dirty dishes and through a weedy garden to a shed at the end. She opened the door. "I havenae touched anything else," she said. "I only took out three gowns for the boys."

"We cannae touch them until a forensic team gets here," said Hamish. He phoned headquarters and got through to Fiona.

"Good work," she said. "Stay there until I arrive."

They retreated into the house. Hamish gave the boys five pounds and they scampered off. "Do you just have the one son?" asked Charlie.

"Aye, Sean."

"Right, let's sit down and take your statement, and then after the forensic team arrive, we'll go up to the moors and you tell us where you found the cases. When did you find them?"

"The Sunday morning, afore they found that body."

"And didn't you think it might be evidence?"

"I just thought some tourist had chucked them. Honest. I put them in the shed. I thought I'd wait to hear if anyone was asking for them. But my boy wanted to go out guising and I thought it wouldnae dae any harm just to let Sean and his pals have three frocks."

*   *   *

At long last, the contingent from Strathbane arrived, headed by Fiona. "We'll go and look for where the suitcases were found," she said, "and leave the forensic team to do their work. But first, we'll need to take your fingerprints, Mrs. Eskdale."

"Ochone, ochone!" she wailed. "It wasnae me who murdered the lassie."

"It is just to eliminate you from our enquiries," said Charlie.

After her fingerprints had been taken, she was told that once they had visited the place where the suitcases had been found, she would be taken to the police station in Lochdubh to make a statement.

As they all left, Fiona taking Mrs. Eskdale in her car, Hamish watched the forensic team suiting up. "Where's Christine Dalray?" wondered Hamish, remembering the attractive forensic scientist who had been keen on him, and wondering why he had never encouraged her.

"I heard she had gone to Glasgow," said Charlie.

Children in all sorts of costumes and carrying turnip lanterns could be seen in the streets.

"I forgot to ask her what she was doing up on
the moors," said Hamish. "She doesnae have a
dog."

Following Fiona's Land Rover, they soon left
the road and bumped across the moors to
where great boulders left since the ice age
loomed up in their headlights. Fiona stopped
beside two of the largest boulders and Hamish
pulled in behind her. They shone powerful
torches into a space between the rocks.

"Found them right there," said Mrs. Eskdale.

"Nothing here that I can see," said Fiona.
"You'd better get back here at daylight, Macbeth. I'll get the forensic boys up here when
they're finished with the house."

"What were you doing, walking up here,
Mrs. Eskdale?" asked Hamish.

"Cannae a body go for a walk?" she
screeched.

Hamish bent down suddenly and picked up
something and held it aloft. "This is a roach.
Do you come up here to smoke pot?"

"That's no' mine!"

"Mrs. Eskdale," said Hamish patiently, "if you say it isn't yours and we have to take it back to get it checked for DNA and find it is yours, you'll be in bad trouble."

She began to wail that she had bad arthritis and there was no harm in a bit of weed.

After more diligent questioning, she revealed she had got it from a neighbour, Hetty Jamieson, who grew a wee bit.

Fiona phoned and ordered a raid on Hetty Jamieson's house before ordering Hamish and Charlie to take Mrs. Eskdale off to Lochdubh to type out a statement.

By the time they had taken the long road back to Lochdubh and got the statement and had run Mrs. Eskdale back to her home, Hamish and Charlie were weary.

They found that Hetty Jamieson had a whole cannabis field covered over in glass and heated in her back garden. She had broken down and said it was some nice Chinese gentlemen who were paying her to look after the crop. They were due the following week to check on it. But as the local press were on the scene, Hamish doubted any Chinese would turn up.

Hamish missed Dick Fraser. Dick would have produced a tent and sleeping bags so that they would be fresh and ready to search the next day. But it was back to the station again for Hamish after dropping Charlie at the hotel.

Hamish was just gulping down a cup of coffee the following morning when Detective Chief Inspector Blair marched into the kitchen.

"You've got to help me," he said. "Thon bloody woman's trying to get me fired."

"Why should I help you?" demanded Hamish. "All you've ever done is to try to get me out of this police station."

Blair gave an oily smile. "Ah, weel. Let's make bygones be bygones. You help me and I'll make sure you keep this poxy station to the end o' time. I want you to say she's been sexually harassing you."

"I've a better idea, sir," said Hamish. "I'll put in a report that *you've* been sexually harassing me."

"You cheeky teuchter! As if anyone would believe you."

"Worth a try. Got to get off. Police work."

"Watch your back from now on, laddie. You've made a bad enemy."

"You always were a bad enemy," said Hamish.

Sonsie let out a hiss and crept towards Blair, her fur raised, while Lugs began to growl.

Blair let out a yelp of alarm and rushed out of the door.

Hamish and Charlie arrived back at the giant boulders where the cases had been found. "This heather's God's gift to criminals," grumbled Hamish. "A truck could run across the stuff and not leave a trace. I don't know what we're doing here. Forensics will make sure there's nothing left to be found."

"I wouldn't be too sure of that," said Charlie. "Since that Christine woman left, they've all gone back to their sloppy ways."

Hamish was hungry and missed Dick again. Dick would have had sausages frying on the camper stove and a flask of coffee. It was a clear frosty morning. Sonsie and Lugs were chasing each other through the heather.

"I wonder how her cap got in the sea," said Charlie.

"Probably blew away when she was shoved ower the cliff," said Hamish.

The sun shone into the space between the boulders and something in a cranny sparkled. Hamish went forward, put on latex gloves, and gingerly fished it out. It was a diamond necklace, a small diamond on a thin, gold chain. "Take a look at this, Charlie."

Charlie came forward. "Maybe the murderer had decided to keep it and then decided to hide it and maybe pick it up later."

Hamish fished out an evidence bag and dropped the pendant into it. "I wonder what she was wearing when she was murdered."

"I mind the inspector telling me. She was wearing a short black dress."

"Not her nurse's uniform?"

"No."

"We'll need to question the Eskdale

woman again. It could be Sean and his friends were looking for outfits and played with the cap and then threw it away. Let's eat something first."

They sat outside the café, eating ham rolls and drinking coffee. "You wouldnae think it was November already," said Charlie.

The incoming tide crashed on the beach and the restless seagulls swooped and dived.

"The only thing I miss in my diet is guga. I could murder a guga," said Charlie.

"Baby gannets? I tried one once," said Hamish. "Didnae fancy it. Oh, well, let's face Mrs. Eskdale."

It transpired that Sean and his friends had tried on the cap and the nurse's uniform found in one of the cases. Sean had gone out wearing the cap. It had blown into the sea. He had gone after it and got it back.

Hamish then phoned Jimmy and told him about the find of the pendant and that it looked as if Gloria had dressed up to go out on a date and then was murdered.

"I'd better get back to Harrison's," said Jimmy. "It's all beginning to look as if the woman was murdered at his place."

"But forensics found nothing," Hamish pointed out.

"I just feel like rattling the cage. If Gloria came on to all and sundry, then she may have made a pass at Juris. You pair, over to Strathbane and hand over that pendant. I'll tell Iron Knickers you're coming."

"I hate going to Strathbane," grumbled Charlie when Hamish had told him what Jimmy had said. "I'm always frightened they won't let me go back to Lochdubh."

When they had passed over the pendant to forensics to check for fingerprints, Hamish and Charlie were just about to leave when Blair approached them. "Not so fast, laddies," he said. "The super wants to see you."

"Now what?" said Hamish. "Blair's been up to something nasty."

They climbed the stairs to Daviot's office. "You are to go right in," said his secretary,

Helen, with a smile that did not reach her eyes. She detested Hamish.

"Ah, come in, come in," said Mr. Daviot. "No, don't stand. Make yourselves comfortable. Tea?"

"Thank you, sir," said Hamish, who didn't want tea but who knew it would infuriate Helen. Daviot summoned Helen. "Tea all round," he said, "and a few Tunnock's tea cakes would go down well."

"Certainly, sir," said Helen. Hamish had placed his cap on the floor beside his chair. Helen managed to tread on it on her road out.

"Don't look so anxious, Macbeth," said the superintendent. "Your station is safe. The matter in hand concerns Constable Carter here."

So that's the way the wind is blowing, thought Hamish wearily. Blair can't get at me but he can get at Charlie.

"The fact is that we are seriously undermanned here. It has been pointed out to me—"

"By Mr. Blair," said Hamish.

"Don't interrupt," snapped Daviot. "Ah. Tea. Thank you, Helen. We'll help ourselves."

✳   ✳   ✳

Downstairs, Fiona was accosted by Blair. "Grand day," he said.

"Have Carter and Macbeth left?" she asked.

"They're up there with the super," said Blair. As Fiona marched towards the stairs, he called after her, "I wouldnae interrupt, if I were you."

Charlie sat, looking stricken. Daviot had just told him he was being transferred back to Strathbane.

The door opened and Fiona walked in. "Ah, Inspector Herring," said Daviot nervously. "Is it very important?"

"When Mr. Blair has a smile all over his fat face," said Fiona, "I assume he has put the boot in for this pair. What's happening?"

"This is an internal matter and nothing to do with you," said Daviot loftily.

Fiona looked at Charlie's miserable face. "Who found that pendant our famous forensic team missed completely?"

"Charlie found it," lied Hamish. "Got an eagle eye when it comes tae clues, ma'am."

"The press are hammering at the doors

demanding a solution to this murder," said Fiona. "So what's going on?"

"We are understaffed," said Daviot. "I have just told Carter he is being transferred to Strathbane."

"Like Macbeth, this constable has been helping me with the investigation," said Fiona, looming over Daviot. "Have you any idea of the enormous extent of Macbeth's beat? One detective chief inspector has stooped to spite. I do not know why you listened to him."

"It was my idea," lied Daviot.

"Very well. I want you to write me a report for the commissioner on why you are removing a constable who knows the area and knows the locals back there."

"I may have been overhasty," blustered Daviot. "Have a tea cake."

"I don't want one. I need this pair with me."

"I feel now I have been overhasty. By all means, Carter, stay in Lochdubh."

"Good," snapped Fiona. "Come along, you pair."

Helen jumped back from the door where she

had been listening. Charlie and Hamish followed Fiona down the stairs.

Blair was waiting at the bottom. Fiona ignored him. "Right," she said, "Charlie, you come with me in my car and Macbeth can follow. We'll go to the station in Lochdubh and go over everything we've got."

Charlie sat in the back of the unmarked police car with Fiona as her driver bore them out of Strathbane. "I am very grateful to you, ma'am," he said.

She smiled and put a hand on his arm. "You are too useful to be got rid of."

Charlie felt as if an electric shock had just gone through his arm. He stared at Fiona. who stared back and then abruptly took her arm away and looked out of the window.

In the police station, Hamish lit the wood-burning stove and put the kettle on top to boil. Fiona looked amused. "Did you never hear of electric kettles, Macbeth?"

"Aye, but Dick Fraser took the kettle away when he moved. I like the stove."

"But I see you have central heating."

"Yes, ma'am. But it's awfy drying. Cosy in here. After we have a coffee, I'll spread out the notes on the table."

Sonsie approached Fiona and stared up at her. Fiona bent down and scratched the cat behind the ears. She began to purr.

"What a huge beast," said Fiona. "Looks like a wild cat."

"Och, no," said Hamish quickly. "Chust a big tabby."

"If you say so."

Hamish made three mugs of coffee and produced a plate of shortbread. "Right," said Fiona, "before we get down to the paperwork, let's see what we know. The late Gloria was a gold digger. None of the men she is believed to have had a fling with was anywhere near the Highlands at the time of her death. So the focus is on Harrison's place until we find anything else."

"If I may make a suggestion, ma'am," said Charlie.

Fiona gave him a warm smile, which transformed the usual hardness of her face.

Oho! thought Hamish, his highland radar twitching. What goes on here?

But before Charlie could speak, the kitchen door opened and Priscilla breezed in.

"Oh, good, coffee," she said. "How are you, Charlie?"

"Who are you?" demanded Fiona, surveying the beauty that was Priscilla.

"I am Priscilla Halburton-Smythe. And you are?"

"I am Inspector Herring and we are discussing a case. So if you don't mind clearing off."

Priscilla shrugged. "See you tonight at dinner, Charlie," she said. "I'm only up on a flying visit."

When she had left, Fiona said, "You were about to say something, Charlie."

"What if it wasnae money?" said Charlie. "What if she was a nymphomaniac? There's other folk up at the box. There's a gamekeeper, Harry Mackay, and a shepherd, Tom Stirling."

"How did you find that out?"

"Asking around."

"Jimmy Anderson is at Harrison's," said Hamish.

"I'd better phone him. And it's too big a place for Inga to do the cleaning all by herself. If there's a cleaning woman, she might have a bit of gossip. Harrison is now denying he said Gloria had gone for a walk and Juris is now saying he might have been mistaken."

She phoned Jimmy and rapped out instructions and, when she had rung off, took a computer out of its case and put it on the kitchen table. "Right! Let's see what we have so far. No fingerprints on that diamond pendant."

Hamish brought in a sheaf of notes from the office.

"She might have been killed by a woman," said Hamish at last. "Gloria might have been messing around with someone's husband. Or, I'm beginning to wonder, was she as bad as she's been painted? Now, I see from the notes that all these men she had dinner with swear blind that was all. They're all married, of course. We have only the maid Elsie Dunbar's word for it. Maybe it just amused Gloria to get free dinners in a posh hotel. Just so long as we go on thinking of her as some sort of tart, we'll be swamped wi' suspects."

"But why would Elsie lie?" asked Charlie.

"Maybe her boyfriend works at the hotel and got sweet on Gloria. I'd like to question her again."

"I'll go, if you like," said Charlie.

"No!" said Fiona with unnecessary force. "You go now, Macbeth."

Hamish left with his pets following at his heels.

At the hotel, Priscilla was in the gift shop and saw him driving up and ran out to meet him. "What a horrible woman!" she exclaimed.

"Oh, herself is all right," said Hamish awkwardly. "I'd like another word wi' that maid, Elsie Dunbar."

"I'll see if she's still in the hotel. Wait in reception."

After a few minutes, Priscilla reappeared with Elsie in tow.

"Now, Elsie," said Hamish, "let's go into the

lounge and sit down. I'd like to go over your statement again."

"I've said all I've got to say," said Elsie stubbornly.

"Aye? Just a few more wee questions."

When they were settled in a corner of the lounge, Hamish studied her mulish face and then said gently, "I know you were lying. And that's a crime. Defeating the ends of justice can mean a prison sentence. So let's have the real story."

Elsie began to sob. Hamish waited patiently until she had dried her eyes and said, "If you tell the truth now, I'll make sure no charges are laid against you."

She twisted her sodden handkerchief between her fingers. "My boyfriend, Graham Southey, works in the bar. She was always flirting with him and he was not charging her for drinks. I was sure he was going to propose, but after Gloria started her tricks, he stopped dating me. I hated the bitch. I wanted everyone to know she was nothing but a cheap hoor."

"So you lied," said Hamish.

She nodded dumbly.

"And to your knowledge, did she ever go upstairs to any of the bedrooms?"

Elsie shook her head.

"No evidence in any of the beds that there had been any malarkey?"

"No, sir. I'm right sorry."

"I'll see what I can do, but don't ever lie to the police again."

When Hamish reported back to Fiona, she said furiously, "Why haven't you arrested her?"

"It's like this," said Hamish wearily. "The lassie would have a criminal record. I understand why she lied. You see, ma'am, up here, it's better to sort out these things without hauling people off to prison. That way, they feel safe to tell me things they might not otherwise think of doing."

"It is a good way of doing things," said Charlie gently. "You see, the way things usually go, if Macbeth sends over a report, Mr. Blair will get his hands on it and before you know it, the lassie will be dragged in and accused of murder.

Mr. Daviot is under such strong pressure from the press that he'll go along with it."

"Surely not!"

"It's happened in other cases," said Hamish.

"I'll let it go for now. Now, Anderson called while you were out. The gamekeeper, Harry Mackay, said he called in at the kitchen with a brace of pheasant just before she was murdered. She was twirling round the kitchen, laughing and singing and saying she was going to be rich. But she didn't say how or why."

"I wonder if the seer knows anything," said Hamish.

"Good God!" exclaimed Fiona. "Are you going to consult the spirits?"

"It's Angus Macdonald. He relies on a lot of local gossip so that it looks as if he knows everything. I'd better take him a present. I've a box of shortbread. That'll do."

"We'll all go and see this Angus," said Fiona. "I'm intrigued."

"We'd better all go in my Land Rover," said Hamish. "Otherwise, it's a steep climb up the brae."

Angus opened the door as they arrived. "He certainly looks the part," remarked Fiona.

"Looks daft," muttered Hamish. For Angus's latest addition to his wardrobe was a long white gown decorated with silver moons and stars. His grey beard seemed to have grown even longer.

"Sorry to have got ye out o' bed," said Hamish maliciously.

Angus ignored him. "Come ben, Miss Herring," he crooned.

Fiona walked in and Angus slammed the door in Hamish's face.

"You shouldnae have hurt the auld man's feelings," said Charlie.

"I'll hurt more than that if he goes on like this." Hamish opened the door and he and Charlie walked in.

"Sit by the fire," Angus was saying to Fiona. "It is the grand thing to have an experienced police officer in Lochdubh. If that is that cheap shortbread from Patel's, Macbeth, put it in the kitchen."

Hamish walked to the kitchen, ducking his

head under the low beams. A lit cigarette was burning in an ashtray on the counter. I didn't know the auld fool smoked, thought Hamish. Although he had given up smoking some time ago, he suddenly felt a sharp longing to pick up that cigarette and take just one puff. He shook his head angrily, stubbed the cigarette out, and returned to the living room.

"So have you heard anything?" Fiona was demanding.

"I will need to consult the spirits." Angus closed his eyes. Hamish stared at him in irritation, but Charlie was wide-eyed.

"It is the money," crooned Angus. "Thon nurse meant to get the old man to marry her. But he found out about her peddling her arse and they had a row. He got an anonymous letter."

"Who told you that?" snapped Hamish.

Angus opened his eyes. "Now you've scared the spirits away."

"I am afraid we will need to take you in for questioning," said Fiona.

The seer's eyes suddenly held a mean look.

"I wonder what your husband would say to that?"

Fiona turned scarlet and Charlie looked shocked. Hamish looked quickly from one to the other.

"May I have a word with you outside, ma'am?" said Hamish.

Fiona followed him outside. "You take that fraud in and I'll tell you what will happen. Folk in Sutherland believe he has the gift. It'll be meat and drink to the newspapers because, trust me, Angus will call a press conference. During that conference, he will get a visit from the spirits, and if there is anything in your private life you do not want made public, then he will broadcast it. People come to him from all over and he has a gift of picking up juicy gossip."

"How do I stop him?"

"Leave him alone in future. But he's given us something to go on. Someone from Harrison's must have spilled the beans. We've got to interview Harrison again."

Inside the cottage, Charlie was looming over

the seer. "If you ever say anything to upset that lady again," he said, "I will break your neck." Then he turned and stalked out, crashing the door shut behind him.

Hamish remained tactfully silent. It was not his business to ask a senior officer about her private life. But when he had said all that about Angus maybe holding a press conference and maybe revealing details of Fiona's private life, he had noticed a flash of fear in her eyes. And was there anything going on between Charlie and Fiona? She must command great respect to be allowed to investigate murder along with two local coppers.

He almost missed Blair. Blair's interference and insults usually spurred Hamish on to greater efforts.

A damp mist was settling down over the countryside. The stunted trees of Sutherland, blasted to near extinction by the severity of the gales, occasionally loomed up at the side of the road in the headlights like crouching old men. Hamish was driving. He had said bad weather was forecast and they would all be safer in the Land Rover.

As he swung in at the gates, a wind sprang up and the fog shifted and danced in front of them. Then the Gothic horror that was the hunting box appeared out of the mist.

"Castle Doom," said Hamish. "Here we are again."

Chapter Five

But onwards—always onwards,
In silence and in gloom,
The dreary pageant laboured,
Till it reached the house of doom.

—William Edmondstoune
Aytoun

As they waited for the door to be opened, Hamish felt suddenly weary. He had a longing for his usually lazy life. He wondered what it would be like to stop being a policeman, buy a bit of land, and become a crofter instead. But as the door opened, a cynical voice in his head said, Buy land? With what?

Juris stood looking at them. "I don't know if I should let you in," he said. "The master is in a fair taking because of that detective who came earlier. He had to stop me being arrested. It was a Detective Chief Inspector Blair and he said, quote, 'Them damn immigrants are the curse o' this country and I am taking your Latvian back to headquarters for questioning.'"

"Stay in the hall," snapped Fiona. "I have urgent calls to make."

Hamish and Charlie waited under the glassy stare of the stuffed heads. "This'll be the end of Blair," said Charlie gleefully.

"Don't bank on it," said Hamish. "That cheil would wangle his way out o' anything."

Fiona came back in. "Juris, that detective had no authority being here. I can only apologise on behalf of the police force. Please explain matters to Mr. Harrison and say we have only a few questions to ask."

After only a few minutes, the nurse, Helen Mackenzie, appeared. She was wearing her usual blue dress with a white collar and cuffs, thick black stockings, and flat, lace-up shoes with thick rubber soles.

"Only a few minutes," she warned. They followed her into the room with the French windows where Hamish had been before.

Mr. Harrison was seated in his wheelchair with a tartan rug over his knees. "Now what is it?" he barked.

"We believe you received an anonymous letter from someone, saying that Miss Dainty hoped to marry you and was after your money. And that she was chasing other men. Do you still have that letter?"

"I burnt it."

"Now, that is a pity. You had a row with her on the night she disappeared, did you not?"

"I'll fire that Latvian!"

"It was nothing to do with Juris."

"So who told you?"

"We cannot reveal our source. Did you have a row with her or not?"

"So what if I did? How the hell do you think a poor cripple like me could strangle the girl, take her to the cliffs, and throw her over?"

"How did you know she was strangled, sir?" asked Hamish. "That was never in the newspapers."

"This is the Highlands, or did you forget, laddie? Gossip, gossip, gossip. I think by now the whole o' Sutherland knows how she died."

"You said to Juris that Gloria Dainty had gone out for a walk. Had she?"

"I don't know. She wasn't around."

"Have your fingerprints been taken?" asked Fiona.

"No, they haven't. I'm tired. Show them out, Mackenzie."

"Either we take them here or you will come with us to Strathbane."

"Get Andrew in here," barked Mr. Harrison. "He's in the library. Andrew is my son and he's a lawyer."

"Under Scots law," said Fiona, "you cannot ask for a lawyer until we say you can."

The door opened and a tall man walked in. He had a large white face, a large nose, and a small pursed mouth. He was completely bald.

He was dressed formally in a charcoal-grey suit and striped shirt with a silk tie.

"What is going on, Father?" he asked. His voice was plummy.

"These coppers want to take my fingerprints."

"It is simply a process of elimination," said Fiona.

"Get a warrant, dear lady," said Andrew. "I have already phoned Superintendent Daviot and put in a complaint. This is police harassment."

"When did you arrive?" asked Hamish.

"Yesterday, with my wife, Greta. I practise in London, and no, I was not up in the Highlands strangling a nurse. Now, if that is all, please leave."

Outside, Hamish asked, "Do you think you can get a warrant?"

"If Mr. Harrison was Jock McSporran, a crofter, I'd get it like a shot. But there's still a lot of class snobbery around, so I doubt if I'll get the permission."

"But why didn't the forensic boys take the old fool's prints?"

"They got Juris, his wife, the new nurse, the cleaner, the gamekeeper, and the shepherd. Harrison probably claimed to be ill."

"I've an idea!" said Hamish. "Wait here."

Before Fiona could protest, he darted off. The wind was getting stronger, soughing through the heather like the sound of the sea. He was glad that Harrison was not interested in gardening, because although there was a lawn at the front, the side and back of the house, along which Hamish silently made his way, were thick with heather. He saw a large square of light from the French windows and crept up. There was one large rhododendron bush by the windows. Hamish stood behind it and leaned forward.

Andrew, Mr. Harrison, and the nurse were there, all laughing at something. Then Mr. Harrison threw aside the tartan rug. He slowly rose to his feet and made his way to a tray of drinks, where he poured himself a large whisky.

Why have I stuck with this mobile dinosaur phone? mourned Hamish. Why didn't I have one of the ones that take photographs? And I left my iPad back at the station.

He made his way swiftly back to where Fiona was impatiently waiting. "What do you think you are doing, Macbeth?" she demanded angrily. "You have no right to—"

"The auld bugger can walk!" said Hamish.

"What?"

"I crept round and looked in the windows and he threw aside his rug, got to his feet, and helped himself to a whisky."

"Now I'll get a warrant, and for his DNA as well. Let's go. I'm hungry."

"There's a good restaurant in Lochdubh," said Hamish.

"Right. That'll do."

"I have a dinner date," said Charlie.

"Cancel it," ordered Fiona.

Blair stood miserably in front of Daviot's desk. "I've had one rocket after another. What the hell were you thinking of? You are suspended from...oh, what is it, Helen?"

"Your wife's on the phone."

Still glaring at Blair, Daviot picked up the phone. "Darling," his wife cooed. "To think I thought you had forgotten my birthday. French perfume and red roses! And such a lovely card. I'm making your favourite dinner tonight. Kiss, kiss!"

Daviot had in fact forgotten her birthday. "Did you send birthday presents to my wife?" he asked Blair when he had rung off.

"I thought you might ha' forgot," said Blair, all fake humility.

"That is very kind of you," said Daviot, thinking of the tremendous and tearful row that Blair had saved him from. "Look, we will say no more about this. Leave the investigation to Miss Herring."

"Where is our Charlie?" demanded the colonel at dinner that night.

"Still working," said Priscilla.

"You know, my dear, I am not a snob."

"Of course not," said Priscilla, suppressing a smile.

"He's a thoroughly decent lad. I would be proud to have him for a son-in-law."

"Not much chance of romance up here," said

Priscilla. "I'm off to London tomorrow. I see Elspeth Grant and her television team have arrived."

Elspeth was furious at being once more taken off her job as presenter to report on the murder. She was always uneasy when she was away from Glasgow, fearing that she might return and find someone had pinched her job.

Priscilla waved to her. Don't see any rings, thought Elspeth. Wonder if Hamish is still hankering after her. After dinner, her crew headed off to bed, but Elspeth felt restless and decided to go to the bar for a nightcap. As she was crossing the entrance hall, a giant of a policeman in uniform walked across the hall and disappeared behind a screen at the far corner.

Curious, Elspeth walked behind the screen and found herself facing a door. She opened it and walked down the steps. She found herself in a musty unlit basement, stumbled over a trunk, and cursed loudly.

A door opened at the far end and the tall

figure of the policeman loomed up against the light. "Who's there?" he demanded.

"A friend of Hamish Macbeth," said Elspeth. "I'm Elspeth Grant."

She walked forward. Charlie stood aside to let her enter his apartment.

"Is this yours?" asked Elspeth, looking around.

"I'm too big for the police station," said Charlie. "Oh, you're thon woman from the telly. You're not to tell anyone about this."

"I can see the headlines now," said Elspeth. "Policeman lives in hotel basement. Don't be daft." She looked up at him in sudden dismay. "You haven't replaced Hamish, have you?"

"Come ben. Take a seat by the fire. No, no, I'm Hamish's constable. I mind now, you used to work up here and you're a great friend o' Hamish's."

"You've made yourself very cosy," said Elspeth.

"Funny. I don't break anything here. I'm right clumsy usually. Drove Hamish mad. A dram?"

"Yes, thanks."

Elspeth relaxed in her chair. There was

something soothing about the big, fair-haired policeman with his lilting accent. "You're from the isles, aren't you?" she said.

"South Uist."

"And how do you like Lochdubh?"

"Oh, it's the grand place." He handed her a glass of whisky.

"I am surprised the colonel allows you to stay here."

"Oh, George is a grand fellow. We go fishing together."

"George! I thought that fussy little snob would never allow anyone to call him anything but Colonel."

"He is the grand man and I won't hear a word against him," said Charlie severely.

"Thanks for the drink," said Elspeth. "I'll be off."

Hamish was just getting ready for bed when he heard a knock at the kitchen door. Lugs gave his welcome bark but Sonsie's fur was raised.

He opened the door and looked down at Elspeth. It was a damp drizzly evening and her hair had frizzed up, making her look more like the old Elspeth he had once known.

"Come in," said Hamish. "Want a dram?"

"Already had one with your constable."

Hamish's hazel eyes sharpened. He was beginning to learn that there was something about Charlie which attracted women.

"So he's living in the hotel basement and seems to be dear friends with the colonel," said Elspeth. "Wonders will never cease. So what about this murder?"

"Off the record?"

"You know me, Hamish."

"Aye, well, I wouldnae mind going over it." Hamish reflected that he had been uneasy during dinner. There was an electricity between Fiona and Charlie. He didn't want Charlie getting hurt and he had been unable to concentrate.

He told her all they had found out. "It's too like a Hollywood movie," commented Elspeth when he had finished. "You know, it's always the one in the wheelchair that no one suspects is able to walk. When are you going back there?"

"I'm to be there at ten in the morning," said Hamish.

Good, thought Elspeth, I'll be there before nine.

Aloud, she said, "So Dick Fraser and Anka have become bap celebrities. I might call in on them. Married yet?"

"Dinnae be daft."

"He might surprise you."

Before he retired to bed, Hamish remembered he had forgotten to check for messages. There were two angry ones from local papers, claiming that the gamekeeper, Harry Mackay, had fired on them.

Elspeth won't get very far, thought Hamish.

But Hamish had forgotten about the magic of television. As the television van rolled up the drive, the crew were confronted by Harry, holding a shotgun on them. The van stopped and Elspeth got down.

"Harry Mackay," she said. "Don't you remember me?"

Harry lowered his gun and grinned. "Why, if

it isnae yourself, Miss Grant. But Mr. Harrison is sore agin the press."

"Oh, he'll see us," said Elspeth. "But before that, would you mind if I interviewed you?"

"Me?"

"You'd look good on film, Harry."

Harry preened. "Maybe chust a few wee words."

So everything was set up and Harry stated that it was a black day for the Highlands and it was his job to protect the estate. All the time, Elspeth fretted, anxious to get to the house before the police arrived.

At last they got to the front door.

Inga answered it but said firmly that Mr. Harrison was not seeing anyone. But Helen Mackenzie appeared and asked what was going on.

"I am Elspeth Grant and I wanted to interview Mr. Harrison and yourself, of course. It is Miss Mackenzie, is it not?"

"Well, I'll see," said Helen. "Wait in the hall."

Ten minutes later, Helen reappeared. She had put heavy make-up on her face and her mouth was a scarlet slash. As she had a long thin mouth, it looked like an open wound made by a razor.

"Just follow me," she said.

It was soon revealed that Helen had spent the time putting on make-up rather than asking Mr. Harrison for his permission.

"What the hell is going on, Mackenzie?" he roared. "I said, no press."

"But it isn't the press, it's the telly," begged Helen.

Andrew Harrison walked into the room. "Ah, Andrew, see these damn folk off the premises," said Mr. Harrison.

"It's just a short interview," pleaded Elspeth.

Andrew surveyed her. Elspeth had straightened her hair and was cleverly made up. Her large silvery eyes looked up into Andrew's face. He smiled. "Father, it'll only take a few moments. I'll get Greta. We don't get much excitement up here and my poor wife is bored."

Sound and camera were already setting up lights and cables. Helen took up a position behind her boss's wheelchair and tried to look solicitous.

Mr. Harrison sat glaring. Greta appeared, followed by her husband. She was a tall woman with a mannish, craggy face and hunting shoulders, wearing a shooting jacket and knee breeches.

"Gosh, isn't this exciting?" she cried. "When will it be shown?"

"At six this evening," said Elspeth. Greta went to stand behind her father-in-law's chair, elbowing Helen out of the way.

Elspeth decided to go straight into the interview and do her piece to camera later.

"Mr. Harrison," she began. "It must have been a dreadful shock when you learned that your previous nurse, Gloria Dainty, had been murdered."

"The little tart had been asking for it," said Mr. Harrison. "Peddling her arse about the Highlands."

"Did you know about her behaviour before she disappeared?"

"Got an anonymous letter and checked

around. Told her to pack up and leave. Thought she had when her stuff was gone."

"Why didn't you tell the police about the anonymous letter?"

"It made me mad and I took it out on Gloria. But then I thought, I wasn't going to blacken her name."

Andrew, Greta, and Helen were now lined up behind Mr. Harrison's wheelchair, all smiling madly at the camera.

"Could you all look a bit serious?" pleaded Elspeth. "Now, Mr. Harrison, can you think of anyone who might have done this dreadful murder?"

He gave a bark of laughter. "Could be anyone. Can't be me. I can't move from this chair."

The door opened and Juris came in. "The police are here with a warrant."

"I'll see them," said Andrew.

"We'd better pack up," said Elspeth. "Thank you all for your time."

Andrew came back. "They've got a warrant,

Father, to take your DNA and fingerprints and also to search the house again."

"This is an outrage! Here I am, a cripple, and being tormented by the fascist police. I'll write to my member of Parliament."

Elspeth had covertly signalled to her crew to keep on filming. "Andrew, what's the use of having a son who's a lawyer when he can do bugger-all to protect me? You always were useless," roared his father.

"I'll get your medicine," said Helen.

Mr. Harrison told her to take the medicine and shove it where the sun didn't shine.

"They're still filming," warned Andrew. Mr. Harrison picked up a medicine bottle from the table next to him and hurled it at Elspeth, who ducked.

Her crew began to hurriedly pack things away, afraid he might start throwing more things and damage the equipment. "And phone my lawyer," said Mr. Harrison. "I'm changing my will."

"But I'm your lawyer," said Andrew.

"Didn't know I had another one, hey? It's old Tinety down in Strathbane."

*   *   *

When Elspeth and her crew left the building, it was to find a forensic team suiting up and Charlie and Fiona standing waiting.

"Where's Hamish?" asked Elspeth.

"He turned up with the cat and dog and the inspector here sent him back saying she didn't want animals contaminating the scene."

"How did you get on?" asked Charlie.

"Don't speak to the press," snapped Fiona.

Elspeth shrugged. With any luck, she might meet Hamish on the road back.

They were just leaving the estate when Elspeth recognised Hamish's Land Rover, leaned out the window, and signalled to him to stop.

Both climbed out of their vehicles and met on the road. "I actually got an interview," said Elspeth. "It's going to look odd on film. Rather like the Addams family, all lined up behind the old man's chair. He lied. He said he couldn't move from the chair. Oh, and at the end, he threw a hissy fit and demanded his lawyer."

"His son's a lawyer."

"Doesn't want him. Got one in Strathbane."

"This is getting more like a damn film every minute," said Hamish. "If it were a film, the old sod would be found dead before he could change his will. I checked the alibis this morning. Andrew and his wife were guests of people down in Somerset the weekend of the murder, so that rules them out." He got back into the Land Rover and drove on to join the others.

Just after he arrived, the head of the forensic team came out. "They're all in the drawing room and we've taken their fingerprints and DNA samples. You can interview them."

"Before we go in," said Hamish, "I'd better tell you what Elspeth Grant has found out."

"You should not have spoken to the press without my permission," raged Fiona.

"Elspeth is a good source of information. Listen to this." Hamish told her about Mr. Harrison changing his will.

"These old folk with money can be murderees," said Fiona. "They use their wills as power over people. 'Be nice to me, or I'll cut you out.' Let's go in and see what we can find out."

Just as they were about to enter the drawing room, Fiona stopped short and held up her hand. They could clearly hear Andrew pleading, "But we've always looked out for you, Father. It was your choice to bury yourself up in this godforsaken place. We offered you a home with us."

"Maybe I've been a bit hasty," came Mr. Harrison's voice. "Get me another whisky, Mackenzie, and don't ever bleat on about my high blood pressure again."

Fiona nodded and opened the door and they all walked in. "What now?" demanded Andrew.

"Mr. Harrison misled us when he claimed he could not walk," said Fiona. "Macbeth here thought he saw someone lurking outside the building when we were last here and went to have a look. He saw you, Mr. Harrison, get out of your chair and go to get yourself a drink."

"Police spies, that's what you are," shouted Mr. Harrison. "I can only walk a few yards."

"That is the case," said the nurse, moving to stand between her employer and the police. "I drive him down once a week to Strathbane Hospital for physiotherapy."

"I don't understand," said Fiona. "You said you came off your horse and broke your back. If you had a broken back you would not be able to walk at all."

"I meant I damaged the nerves on my spine," said Mr. Harrison.

Fiona painstakingly took him back through the events of the evening when Gloria had disappeared until Helen Mackenzie stepped forward.

"That's enough," she said harshly. "You have tired him. It's time for his nap. Come along, sir." She seized the handles of his wheelchair and pushed him towards the door, which Andrew leapt to hold open.

When he had gone, Fiona turned her attention to Andrew. "Do you know what is in his will?"

"He said he had some lawyer in Strathbane," said Andrew, "but as far as I know, I am the heir."

"And what is the name of the lawyer in Strathbane?"

"Someone called Tinety, I think."

Hamish left Charlie to take down what was being said while he studied Andrew. Pompous but hardly the murdering type, he thought. Still, it's hard to tell.

When they were once more outside, Fiona phoned Jimmy Anderson and asked him to visit the lawyer in Strathbane and see if he could find anything out. When she rang off, she said to Hamish, "You go back to that cliff. There must be something we missed. Charlie will come with me to Strathbane where he can type up his notes, and then we'll go over what we've got."

As he got into his Land Rover, Hamish watched Charlie and Fiona getting into the back of Fiona's car and pushed his peaked cap back and scratched his fiery-red hair in bewilderment. Fiona must have a lot of power to use the services of a lowly constable like Charlie. Was something going on there? She was married and Charlie was a great big innocent. I hope he doesn't get hurt, thought Hamish.

He drove on up the coast, turning all he knew over in his mind. Gloria had been trying to seduce her employer. Gloria was a gold digger. Therefore it followed that anyone wanting her out of the way would surely be someone like Andrew or his wife, who felt they were about to lose their inheritance. But both were alibied up to the hilt. So that left only old Harrison, furious at finding out she had been playing around. Say he had strangled her in a rage. He could have paid Juris a large sum to dump the body.

Better get Charlie to check his bank accounts. But where does he bank? Should have asked. He realised he was hungry and stopped at the café for a bacon sandwich and a cup of coffee.

The café was quiet. "Do you do much business here?" asked Hamish.

"We get a lot of folk in the summer. I'm Sheena Farquar." She was a small, rosy-cheeked, grey-haired woman.

"Hamish Macbeth. Folk must have been

talking a lot about the murder. Did anyone see anything?"

"Only poor auld Jessie McGowan. The girl's daft. But it's believed she has the sight."

Hamish knew she was referring to the second sight, certain highlanders supposedly blessed with seeing the future. Even Boswell and Johnson went searching for evidence of it in their tour of the Hebrides.

"Where does she live?"

"A wee house at the end o' Loan Road. It's got a purple door."

"Does she live alone?"

"Aye, her parents are dead. She can look after herself well enough, but she scares people, always mumbling and talking to herself."

Hamish made his way to Loan Road and located the house with the purple door. There was no doorbell. But there was a brass knocker in the shape of a devil's head. He raised his hand to knock but the door was jerked open.

At first he thought this could surely not be Jessie McGowan, for the small woman looking up at him seemed sane enough.

"I am Police Sergeant Hamish Macbeth," he said. "I would like a few words with Miss McGowan."

She nodded and stood aside to let him enter. There was a tiny square of a hall. She opened a door to the left. Hamish followed her in. It was a conventional living room with a rather battered three-piece suite in brown corduroy, a coffee table, a fireplace with ornaments on the mantelpiece, and lace curtains at the window.

"I am Miss McGowan." She sat down on the edge of one of the armchairs and surveyed him. Despite her long grey hair, he guessed she might be in her late thirties. She was wearing a white Aran sweater over faded jeans. Her long thin face was very white, her grey eyes hooded with thick lids.

"A body was found at the foot of the cliffs," said Hamish, putting his cap on the coffee table. "I believe you might have seen something."

"That I did," she said. Hamish felt hopeful. The woman seemed perfectly sane.

She continued, "It was Auld Nick himself."

Hamish's heart sank. But he asked, "Are you sure it was the devil?"

She nodded. "Describe him," said Hamish.

"All black. Black face, black everything."

"And what was he doing?"

"He was standing on the top of the cliffs, looking down. Then he turned away and disappeared."

"Where were you?"

"I was down on the beach hiding behind a rock. I go there sometimes to talk to the dead. The seals, you know. Folk come back as seals."

"Did you hear the sound of a car or any vehicle?"

She looked at him solemnly out of her odd grey eyes. "Himself just goes back down to the nether regions. When I peeked round the rock again, he had gone."

Hamish thought quickly. It could all be nonsense, or the murderer could have been dressed in black with the face covered by a black balaclava.

"The thing that puzzled me," she said in her

thin voice, "is why he did not take her down to hell."

"Why would he want to do that in the first place?" asked Hamish patiently.

"She caused hatred and fear."

"Did you know the nurse?"

"No, but I saw it all in my mind."

"Pictures or emotions?"

"Feelings. Nasty feelings. And there is more to come. Death is coming."

"Who's going to die?" asked Hamish.

"A man."

"What man?"

"I don't know. Just a man. There is danger surrounding you, Mr. Macbeth."

"From the devil?"

"Often the devil's instruments are human."

She began to rock back and forth, mumbling incomprehensible things. Hamish got to his feet and walked out. He had just reached the front door when her voice stopped him.

"Mr. Macbeth!"

He swung round.

"I have not offered you any tea."

Once more, she looked quite sane.

"Another time," said Hamish, and made his escape.

He drove back to the hunting box to join Fiona, who was standing in the hall, telling her about his odd interview but saying it might be wise to search the house for any black clothing. Two detectives and three policemen who had been searching the house after the forensic team had finished their work and were just packing up were told about Hamish's discovery and told to go back in and look for black clothing.

They were confronted by Andrew. "I thought you had finished here," he said angrily.

"Macbeth's found a witness up at Kinlochbervie, some daft woman with the second sight, who says she saw the killer up on the cliffs. Mind you, she thought it was the devil."

"Oh, I am so sick of all of you. I have complained to the procurator fiscal," said Andrew, and he went into the drawing room to report to the others this latest outrage.

*   *   *

When they all moved outside, Hamish said to Fiona, "What do you hope to get from all the fingerprints and DNA? Was there anything on the body?"

"They can maybe get fingerprints off the neck."

"But they think she was strangled with a scarf or some sort of material."

"Damn. I'd forgotten that."

They were joined by Jimmy Anderson. "I've got heavy expenses," he said. "I had to take that lawyer, Cameron Tinety, out for a lot of drams to get information out of him. He says there was a will leaving everything to Gloria Dainty."

"There's a motive!" exclaimed Fiona.

"But he changed it and said he wanted the old will leaving everything to his son. But it was changed two weeks afore Gloria was murdered."

"Andrew may not have known that," said Charlie. "I'll ask Juris if Andrew had visited the old man before."

He went into the house. "Macbeth," said

Fiona, "tell me exactly what this odd creature said."

Hamish began to talk but she interrupted him. "Didn't you take notes?"

"I was afraid it would put her off, ma'am. But I remember everything she said."

When he had finished, Fiona sighed. "What a load of rubbish. Do you believe in this second sight nonsense?"

"It's awfy hard to prove," said Hamish. "Folk usually tell you they saw whatever coming after it happens."

"There are enough of us here," said Fiona. "Go back to your usual duties, Macbeth."

"Yes, ma'am. I'll wait for Charlie."

"No, leave him here. Anderson, you report back to Strathbane and type up a full report."

Charlie came out to join them. "This was the son's first visit since the old man moved up here."

"We'd better talk to him again," Fiona said with another sigh. "Let's go, Charlie."

Back at the police station, Jimmy followed Hamish in. "Any whisky?"

"I think you've already had a skinful," said Hamish. "You'd best be on your road."

"Thon Fiona has the hots for Charlie."

"But she's married?"

"Aye, and to none other than Lord Staford McBean, high court judge."

"Are you sure? He's in Edinburgh and she's out o' Inverness."

"Sure as sure."

"But she's called Fiona Herring! Not Lady McBean."

"Keeps her maiden name for work. C'mon, laddie, give us a dram. I am your senior officer."

Hamish sighed and took a new bottle of whisky down from a cupboard.

"But she cannae fancy our Charlie," protested Hamish.

"Why not? Big strong fellow like that."

"Well, if that's true, there's one good thing. Our innocent Charlie seems to be woman-proof. Never really notices them. Treats Priscilla like a sister."

Jimmy took a gulp of whisky. "It was a good thing it was you and not Blair interviewing that nutter up in Kinlochbervie. He'd ha' had the lassie sectioned and hauled off to the nut house. Do you believe that second sight stuff?"

"Elspeth Grant sometimes seems able to see things coming."

"Load o' bollocks, if you ask me."

There followed a quiet few days for Hamish. Charlie wasn't even around, Fiona having kept him down at Strathbane going over and over statements. Charlie phoned once saying miserably that he wished the whole sorry business was over because he hated Strathbane and missed Lochdubh and the friendly dinners with the colonel and his wife.

Hamish felt he should be glad to have the police station to himself again. But somehow, he felt lonely. He was just thinking of going to Braikie to see Dick and Anka when the phone rang. It was Fiona, sounding impatient.

"Get back up to Kinlochbervie," she ordered, "and go from door to door. There must be something we've missed."

Hamish was about to point out that the police had already been from door to door, but bit his lip and agreed to go. He whistled to Sonsie and Lugs, put them in the Land Rover, and set off.

He realised he hadn't had any breakfast and decided to stop at the café first. Great mountainous waves were pounding the beach. Black clouds streamed in from the west. The air was full of salt and blowing sand. The gulls were huddled on the cliff shelves and crannies. It seemed as if the whole world were in motion. A rowan tree outside the café tossed its bare branches up as if pleading with the menacing sky.

He pushed open the door and went in. "I was just about to phone you," said Sheena Farquar.

"Why? What's up?" asked Hamish.

"It's that daft lassie, Jessie McGowan. Herself hasnae been seen around. A neighbour knocked at her door but got no reply."

"Have you any idea where she might have gone?" asked Hamish.

"Could be anywhere. Mind you, she was

always mumbling about some fairy cave in the cliffs, but if there was one, the schoolboys would have found it. She said the fairies sang to her."

"I'll have a look," said Hamish, "afore the storm gets worse. Could you make me three bacon sandwiches to go?"

"Right you are. You must be hungry."

Hamish did not want to say that his cat and dog were partial to bacon sandwiches. He drank a cup of coffee while he waited, listening uneasily to the shrieking of the wind.

He climbed into the Land Rover, unwrapped two of the bacon baps and passed them over to Lugs and Sonsie in the back, then ate his own while putting off the moment when he would need to get out and start to search the cliffs.

At last, he took off his cap, knowing the gale would whip it away and he needed both hands if he had to climb.

He stumbled along the sand, past where Gloria's body had been found, becoming increasingly uneasy. They had been inside Harrison's house when he had told Fiona what Jessie had said. Had he put her at risk? A great buffet of wind sent him flying into a tall standing rock and he cursed and rubbed his shoulder. He searched and searched but there was no sign of any cave. He was about to turn back when he heard a weird whistling and moaning sound coming from some way up the cliffs. He screwed up his eyes against the flying sand and dried seaweed. Halfway up the cliff, he saw a dark slit in the rock. He began to climb.

As he grew nearer, he wondered if this was Jessie's fairy cave. The wind was causing unearthly noises to emanate from it, shrill keening sounds that he could hear despite the tumult of the storm. He finally edged his way in through the narrow entrance. It opened up into a cave. He unhitched a torch from his belt and shone it around.

In a corner, crumpled up like a discarded doll, lay the body of Jessie McGowan. He bent over her. There was no pulse. Her face was contorted and there were signs all around that she had vomited. He took out his mobile phone but there was no signal.

His journey down from the cave was perilous as the wind seemed determined to pluck him off the cliff face and throw him into the sea. Worse, the tide was up and he had to battle through breakers until he reached dry land, soaked to the skin. He went into the café and asked for a roll of paper towels.

"How did you get like that?" asked Sheena.

"Jessie's dead." He took out his phone. No signal.

"Use the landline on the counter," said Sheena. "This is awful."

A "weather bomb," as the forecasters now called it, was due to hit the northwest of Scotland. Hamish reflected sourly that one day they might wake up to the fact that hurricane-force winds were becoming more and more frequent.

Fiona, Charlie, and Jimmy were the first to arrive and to find Hamish dressed in the late Mr. McGowan's old sweater and trousers.

"Where is your uniform?" demanded Fiona.

"It's hanging up in the kitchen to dry," said Hamish. "I nearly got drowned on the road back from the cave. We'll need to wait until the tide goes out."

"But we had no trouble getting along the beach to Gloria's body," said Fiona.

"There wasnae a hurricane like this, ma'am," said Hamish.

Jimmy had bought a bottle of whisky. "You look as if you could do with a dram, Hamish," he said.

"Give him one," snapped Fiona, "and then screw the top firmly back on the bottle. How long is this storm due to last?"

"Until this evening," said Hamish.

"And it's already as black as pitch," said Fiona. The café had three tables. She sat down at one and indicated that Charlie should join her. Hamish and Jimmy sat at another table. Fiona ordered coffee for all of them. Jimmy managed to get a slug of whisky into his cup when Fiona wasn't looking.

The procurator fiscal arrived and Fiona settled down to give him a full report.

I actually wish Blair were in on this one, thought Hamish. I'd like to see him trying to get his fat carcase up into that cave.

But Blair was busy plotting the downfall of Fiona.

Chapter Six

The clouds dispell'd, the sky resum'd her light,
And Nature stood, recover'd of her fright,
But fear, the last of ills, remain'd behind,
And horror heavy sat on ev'ry mind.

—Dryden

While Hamish and the rest waited for the full contingent from Strathbane to arrive, Detective Chief Inspector Blair was seated in the grimy office of private detective Willie Dunne.

"I've got a wee job for you, Willie," said Blair. "You'll be paid well if you keep your mouth shut. Remember, I hae the power to shut ye down."

Willie was nicknamed Creepy Willie. He was a small Glaswegian with a comb-over of dyed brown hair on his freckled pate and a face that seemed to be all nose. He specialised in divorces.

"Out wi' it," he said.

"There's this inspector o' police called Fiona Herring. That's her maiden name. She's married to a high court judge, Lord Staford McBean."

"Haud it right there, mac," said Willie. "This is flying too high."

"You'll do it," said Blair, "or I'll have you for dealing drugs out o' this office."

"You wouldnae!"

"Like a shot."

Willie knew of Blair's reputation and that the detective would plant drugs in his office and arrest him if he didn't do what was asked.

"Okay. Out wi' it."

"This Fiona is sweet on a copper called Charlie Carter, based at Lochdubh. He's a big lummox of an islander. I've watched the way she looks at him. I want you to catch them in the act."

"How the hell am I going to get into the polis station in Lochdubh?"

"No need for that. A kiss would be good enough. Does Hamish Macbeth know you?"

"No."

"So I'll map out for you where they are and where they go. You pretend to be a local photographer. Thon bitch is ruining my career."

Blair opened an envelope. "Here's a photo. I snapped it off when they werenae looking."

Willie looked gloomily at the photo. It showed Fiona in her uniform, sitting at a desk. Charlie stood behind her. Fiona, thought Willie, looked as hard as nails.

"So," said Blair, "you'd better start. They're up at a site outside Kinlochbervie. Found another dead body. The press will have gathered by now. The storm's died down."

It was ten in the evening and the winds had charged off to plague the east. The café was open and a flushed and happy Sheena was busy serving food and drinks to the press.

Hamish, in his dry uniform but with newspaper

stuffed inside his still-damp boots, was with Fiona and Charlie, waiting for the forensic team to finish their work. The pathologist, an elderly man brought all the way over from Aberdeen, could not climb up to the cave and was waiting for the body to be stretchered down to where a tent had already been erected to receive it.

"Someone up at that hunting lodge must have heard my report," fretted Hamish.

"We'll get over there when we've got the pathologist's preliminary finding," said Fiona.

"Perhaps Jimmy should go ahead," suggested Hamish.

Fiona rounded on him. "I will do any interviews, Macbeth. Do try to remember who's in charge here. Go and interview the dead woman's neighbours."

"Okay, let's go, Charlie," said Hamish.

"Charlie will stay here with me," said Fiona. "And everyone, keep your voices down. The press are listening."

Before he left, Hamish turned in the doorway and looked at the press. He recognised a few from the provincial papers, but there was one seedy-looking man and Hamish did not like the way he was studying Fiona.

Sheena followed him out and gave him a flask of coffee and a wrapped ham sandwich. "That'll keep you going," she said.

"That's very kind of you," said Hamish.

"Aye, well, it's a pity you're not the one she fancies."

"Are you talking about the inspector?"

"She seems a hard woman, but when she looks at thon Charlie, her face goes all soft."

"Maybe it's just maternal instinct," said Hamish.

"Och, away wi' ye. Thon's a budding romance."

"Have you got a camera?" asked Hamish.

"Aye."

"There's a fellow there wi' the press who disnae seem to belong, a ferrety wee man wi' a big nose and a comb-over. Could you get me a photo of him and e-mail it to me? Here's my card."

"I can do that."

Hamish climbed into the Land Rover and

drove to Kinlochbervie. The first thing he saw were policemen going from door to door. He cursed Fiona but then remembered that Sonsie and Lugs had been locked up in the Land Rover for too long. So he drove up onto the moors and let them out and sat eating the ham sandwich and drinking coffee as his pets ran through the heather.

The trouble with winter in the Highlands, thought Hamish, was that there was so little sunshine, it was like living in long hours of darkness.

He was sure that Jessie had been poisoned. He had said nothing about the fairy cave. How could it have been done? Say someone called on her and Jessie had started to talk about the fairy cave. Maybe a present of a bottle of something and why don't you take some to the fairies? He had not searched the cave. He had backed out quickly so as not to contaminate the crime scene. Would the forensic team have been to her house yet? Would they even know what to look for? He called to his animals and set off full-speed for Jessie's home.

There was no police tape yet outside. He put on his full forensic gear and then tried the door. It wasn't locked. He searched the kitchen first. Two cups and saucers had been washed and were lying on the draining board. He made his way quickly to the living room. He knew he had to be quick. As soon as the neighbours got the news, they would be gathering outside. And he didn't want to be caught by the forensic team. The living room was neat and clean. He was about to turn away when his eye caught something glittering on the floor near the sofa. He bent down and examined it. It was a strand of sparkling ribbon, the kind used to wrap a present.

He hurried out and took off his forensic suit and went to question the neighbours. Had any strangers been seen?

The woman next door said that only a couple of what she described as Bible bashers, a man and a woman, had called the day before. No one else. Their description didn't match anyone that Hamish had seen at the hunting box.

Whoever it had been, thought Hamish, could

have come during the night and left a package on the doorstep. Maybe Jessie had decided to share some treat with her fairies in the cave. Or could it have been suicide? No, he couldn't believe that. She had looked as if she had died in agony. He diligently knocked at doors up and down the street. Jessie had been well liked, considered daft but harmless, and the neighbours were shocked to learn of her death.

More police arrived and started going from door to door. Police tape was put up in front of Jessie's house.

Neighbours gathered in the street, talking in whispers.

Hamish returned to the café to be told by a local reporter that the police had left. Guessing they had gone to Harrison's, he set off. As he was turning into the drive, his iPad clicked. He opened it. There was a message from Sheena. "You ran off before I could catch you. Attached is a photo of the man you're interested in." Hamish clicked on the photo and studied it. Then he moved on to park outside the house.

Fiona, Charlie, and Jimmy were standing out-

side. "Why aren't you at Kinlochbervie?" demanded Fiona.

"Overmanning," said Hamish. "You've already
got the place covered in police. But I've got something to show you." He took out a forensic bag
and held it up. Inside the clear material could be
seen the little sparkly strip of ribbon. Hamish
did not want to say he had found it inside the
house so he said he had found it on the front
doorstep. "If she's been poisoned," he said, "this
could have come off some sort of present, maybe
a bottle of something. She could have taken it
up to her favourite cave, drunk it, and died there.
Any idea what the poison might have been?"

"No," said Fiona wearily. "Andrew Harrison
has pulled so many strings that I've been ordered
by the high-ups to tread carefully. There's not
much we can do until the results of the autopsy
come through. We'll meet here in the morning."

Jimmy followed Hamish into the police station
in Lochdubh, waiting impatiently for whisky
while Hamish lit the stove and put out food
and water for his pets.

"At last," he grumbled when Hamish put the bottle of whisky and a glass on the table.

"I've something to show you," said Hamish. He switched on his iPad and showed Jimmy the photograph Sheena had sent him. "Recognise this man?"

"I've seen him before," said Jimmy. "Gie me a moment. Nothing like whisky to lubricate the brain."

Hamish was sure he had recognised the man immediately and simply wanted an excuse for another drink.

"Aye, I've got it now. Thon's Creepy Willie."

"And who in the name o' the wee man is Creepy Willie?"

"He's a sleazeball o' a private detective. Divorce cases. Think he deals drugs but haven't been able to catch him yet."

Hamish's mind raced. Could Fiona's husband be checking up on her? Hardly. He would employ a reputable man from Edinburgh.

Was there really anything going on between Charlie and Fiona?

"I think it may have something to do with

our boss. I'd better get up to the castle and warn Charlie." He seized the whisky bottle and put it back in the cupboard. "No more, Jimmy, or you won't be fit to drive."

Fiona and Charlie were relaxing in front of the fire in Charlie's apartment. Fiona yawned and stretched. "I feel too tired to go back to Strathbane."

"I can ask the manager to find you a room here," said Charlie.

She smiled at him and said softly, "You have a bed here, Charlie."

Charlie blushed to the roots of his hair. "It is the double bed."

"So? Oh, who the hell is this?"

They could hear someone clattering down the stairs. Charlie jumped to his feet and stood barring the doorway.

"It's yourself, Hamish," he said with relief. "Miss Herring and I were just having a final discussion."

"Look. There's no one in the lounge upstairs. Follow me up. It's urgent."

Fiona had appeared behind Charlie. Silently they followed Hamish upstairs and through to a corner of the hotel lounge.

"There is a private detective who specialises in divorce," said Hamish. "He is checking on you for some reason, ma'am."

"What reason could he have?" said Fiona coldly.

"It can't be anyone employed by your husband," said Hamish. "He would surely not employ such as Willie Dunne, a lowlife from Strathbane. He was at the café earlier and he is now in this hotel."

"I still don't know why you should think this lowlife had anything to do with me," said Fiona angrily.

"I will go now and see if I can get hold of him," said Hamish, "and find out what he's up to."

The porter on reception recognised Willie from Hamish's photograph. "He was asking about Charlie and thon inspector and where were they. I told him to get lost. I followed him to the car park and made sure he left."

Hamish returned to the lounge. Two spots of colour burned on Fiona's cheeks when Hamish reported that Willie had been asking about her and Charlie.

"Don't worry," he said. "I'll call on him tomorrow and shake it out of him."

When Hamish had left, Fiona rose to her feet. Charlie stood up as well. "I'll take a room at the hotel," she said stiffly.

"Does your driver need accommodation?" asked Charlie.

"I dismissed him," she said curtly. "I will meet you at Lochdubh police station in the morning."

Hamish paced restlessly up and down the police station, too worried to go to bed. At last he decided to phone Willie. He found his home number and rang it.

When Willie answered, Hamish said, "Why are you checking up on Inspector Herring? This is Sergeant Macbeth from Lochdubh."

"I'm not," screeched Willie. "I do a wee bit for the papers, see."

"Havers! You were asking questions at the hotel. Who's employing you?"

"I'm telling you. No one!" Willie was terrified that if he gave up Blair, then Blair would find a way to get him arrested. He suddenly saw a way out.

"Thae murders you're on," he said. "I think I ken who's done them. I was thinking o' telling the inspector but I got cold feet."

"Tell me!"

"Come in the morning to the office," said Willie, and hung up.

As soon as he was finished with Hamish, Willie made a call. He spoke rapidly, finishing with, "I don't know if it's you, or not, but I've got to give the police something. Get your passport ready."

Charlie and Fiona arrived at the station to find a note on the table from Hamish. "Gone to see Willie. He says he's got news of our murderer."

"We'd better go as well," said Charlie.

"No," said Fiona sharply. "This station should be manned. You stay here."

She strode out. Sonsie and Lugs stared at Charlie. "Must be serious," said Charlie, "or he would ha' taken you pair. It's a grand day. Let's go for a walk."

As Hamish rounded into the grimy street where Willie had his office, he found his way blocked by police cars and fire engines.

He got out and made his way forward to where Detective Inspector Blair was talking to the fire chief.

Blair scowled at Hamish. "What are you doing here?"

"Willie Dunne told me he had information about the murderer. He told me to call this morning. What's happened here?"

"Too early to tell," said the fire chief.

"And Willie Dunne?"

"Burnt to a crisp."

"Murder?"

"Too early to tell."

"Wait a minute," roared Blair. "This is my case."

Hamish stared at him for a long moment.

Surely if anyone wanted to destroy Fiona's reputation, it would be Blair.

"A word with you, sir," said Hamish, walking a little away. Blair followed him.

"Willie was employed by someone to spy on Miss Herring," he said.

"Rubbish!" roared Blair, turning a muddy colour. "Get oot o' here, ye great daft gowk."

He watched uneasily as Hamish walked away. Thank heavens everything in that office, including Willie, had been burnt to cinders.

Hamish drove up onto the moors. He needed peace and quiet to think. If it had been Blair who had employed Willie, and feared he had been found out, would he go to the lengths of murdering the man? Willie may have phoned Blair during the night and told him that he, Hamish, was on his trail. But murder?

Willie had been just the sort of creature to blackmail some of his clients. What if he had warned the murderer?

Any evidence that might have been in the office was now lost.

His phone rang. It was Fiona. "I have just heard the news about the fire."

"On my road back from it," said Hamish.

"You should have phoned me immediately. Go back to your station and I'll meet you there."

Hamish drove to Lochdubh as fast as he could. It was one of those rare balmy days when a mild west wind blew in from the Gulf Stream. The mountains soared up to a pale-blue sky. He longed for the case to be over.

Fiona was waiting outside the police station. There was no sign of Charlie.

"Where's Charlie?" asked Hamish.

"I have sent him to Kinlochbervie. I asked him to man this station but when I checked, he was out walking those ridiculous pets of yours. He might be able to find out something the other policemen have missed."

They walked into the police station where Hamish gave her a rapid report of his conversation with Willie.

"I think," he concluded by saying, "that Willie was just the sort of lowlife to maybe blackmail his clients. So, say he knew something about someone that might lead us to the identity of the murderer. He was prepared to do that rather than give up the name of whoever asked him to spy on you."

"Have you any idea who might have employed Willie to spy on me?" she asked.

Hamish hesitated only a moment before he said, "I cannae think o' anyone, ma'am."

He knew that if he said he suspected Blair, there would be a full enquiry. He would be asked to present all his suspicions and findings in triplicate and nothing would come of it.

Fiona took out her phone. "I'd better get headquarters to find out the identity of all phone calls to that hunting box last night."

When she had finished, she said, "What on earth are you doing, Macbeth?"

"I'm lighting the stove, ma'am."

"There's no time for that. You get off and join Constable Carter. And don't take your weird animals with you."

He saw Fiona out and waited until she had been driven off, then made his way to his friend Angela Brodie's house.

Angela was the doctor's wife and an author. Hamish often wondered why she bothered to write anything at all because she seemed to hate the process so much. She was seated at a cluttered kitchen table where three cats prowled among the breakfast debris. One had its head in the milk jug.

She smiled at Hamish. "I'm glad to see you. Coffee?"

"No thanks," said Hamish, reflecting that Angela was amazingly unsanitary for a doctor's wife. "One of your cats has its head in the jug and another is licking the butter."

"Shoo!" said Angela, waving her hands. "What do you want, Hamish?"

"I've left Sonsie and Lugs back at the station. I know they frighten your cats so I didn't bring them. But if you could pop in from time to time and see they've got water and food."

"All right. But they'll probably go along to the restaurant kitchen and mooch something. How's the case?"

"Dead, slow, and stop. What do you think of immigrants, Angela?"

"Apart from thinking occasionally that if you took all the Eastern Europeans out of Scotland, the hotels would be self-service, and if you took the Indians and Pakistanis out of the National Health Service, it would collapse?"

"Right. But a lot o' folk complain so much about them that I'm inclined to lean too far the other way," said Hamish. "Now, Juris and Inga Janson are called Latvians. But they are British citizens. In reaction to xenophobia, I haven't been studying them that closely."

Angela had been typing on a laptop at the table. With a sigh of relief, she closed it down and pushed a wisp of hair away from her gentle face.

"You have to ask yourself what the motive is," she said. "Surely, money is the motive."

"In that case, the one that had the most to lose," said Hamish, "would be the son, Andrew, but he's got a cast-iron alibi."

"You always used to say that the ones with cast-iron alibis were suspicious. Oh, do get off, Flopsy." Angela gently removed a fat cat from her computer and put it on the floor.

"Let me think," said Hamish. "Andrew and his wife claim to have been guests of friends in Somerset the weekend of the murder. Maybe they got the friends to lie for them. I'll check it out."

As Hamish had expected, he found Charlie at the café. "It's no use, Hamish. Everyone's been interviewed over and over again and they've got nothing to add. Does anyone know what poisoned her?"

"Too early," said Hamish, sitting down to join him. "Why are you banished from Fiona's side?"

Charlie gave a massive shrug. "Don't know. I think that detective scared her."

"Did you hear about him being killed?"

"Yes, herself briefed me afore sending me off."

"I wish I could get down to England and check out Andrew's alibi."

"I've got my computer in my car," said Charlie. "We can find out their names and make a call. Say something like doubts have been cast on their alibi and the dire consequences of perverting the course of justice."

They walked out to Charlie's old Volvo, one of the long ones that looks like a hearse but is big enough to accommodate his height. They both climbed in. Charlie switched on his laptop and began to scroll through the notes. "Here we are," he said. "Bunty and Jeremy Thripp. Who is going to phone?"

"I'll have a try," said Hamish, "because if Andrew gets to hear we've been checking up on him, someone's going to get it in the neck and it may as well be me."

Hamish took out his phone, squinted at the computer screen, and dialled a number. A woman answered. "Is that Mrs. Thripp?" asked Hamish.

"Yes, but I'm not buying anything."

"This is Police Sergeant Hamish Macbeth from Lochdubh in Sutherland. You and your husband claim that Andrew Harrison and his wife were with you on the weekend a nurse who had been looking after his father was murdered."

"Yes, that's right," she said. "Why are you asking again?"

"Someone has come forward," lied Hamish, "with a suggestion that you may be guilty of perverting the course of justice by giving them an alibi. If this is true, you do realise you will be charged and maybe go to prison?"

"My lawyer will be in touch with you," she shouted, and banged down the phone.

"No good?" asked Charlie.

"Says she'll get her lawyer."

"Are they tapping the calls at the hunting box?"

Hamish shook his head. "The inspector said she couldn't get permission. But look at it this way: Why did she say she would get her lawyer? Why not honest outrage at the very suggestion? We'll wait and see. If nothing at all happens, I'll need to pluck up my courage and tell your inspector what I've done. Inaction would suggest guilt. And if it had been an innocent person getting that call, they would have surely asked for my phone number and called me back to make sure it was me. Finding it was someone

on a mobile, she'd have hung up and called Andrew, who would then call Daviot."

"What do we do now?" asked Charlie.

"Forget about the whole thing until the axe
falls, if it's going to fall. I know. Let's go and see
Dick Fraser at the bakery. No point in hanging around here. It's half day in Braikie, so the
shop'll be closed."

Dick and Anka welcomed them. Charlie's clum-
siness returned. He dropped his coffee cup on
the floor and, bending over to retrieve it, fell on
the carpet. As they all helped him up and Anka
gave him a fresh cup of coffee, Charlie thought
sadly that while he had been with the colonel
or Fiona, he hadn't broken anything at all.

Anka had been working on Internet orders
and excused herself to go through to the office,
leaving Hamish and Charlie with Dick.

Dick eagerly asked how the case was going.
He listened carefully while Hamish talked.
When Hamish had finished, Dick said, "I don't
think it can have anything to do with the son."

"Why?" asked Hamish.

"Look at it this way. If Willie had the goods on someone, it must be someone in Sutherland. He'd hardly know anything about a London lawyer. This Juris: Did Gloria make a pass at him?"

"Yes, according to his wife, who threatened to kill her."

"Or," said Dick, folding his hands over his stomach, "it could be someone out of Gloria's past in Strathbane. You think Willie might have been a blackmailer? Gloria liked money. Maybe she supplied him with the goods on somebody. Maybe no one's dug into her background properly."

"That's a good idea," said Hamish. "I just assumed that our inspector would have found out everything there was to know. Let's see. Gloria worked in Strathbane Hospital before going into private nursing. I'd like to get down to that agency and see who she was taking care of before she got the job with old Harrison."

"We'd better tell the inspector," said Charlie cautiously. "I mean, we're supposed to be in Kinlochbervie."

"I'll try anyway." Hamish phoned Strathbane, but was told that Fiona and Jimmy were back at the hunting lodge. He phoned Fiona's mobile and it went straight to the answering service. So he left a long message about where they were about to go and what they were about to do. He then switched off his own phone and told Charlie to do the same.

Charlie left his car at the police station and joined Hamish in the Land Rover. The sun was crawling reluctantly over the horizon as they drove into Strathbane. The agency, Private Nursing, was in a former villa near the hospital.

Before he rang the bell, Hamish said, "I'd like to interview the nurse that Gloria replaced. She may have known her."

He pushed the round white bell set in brass by the door. It was opened by a thin woman with a haggard face. Hamish explained who they were and what they wanted.

"I am the secretary here, Alexandra Chisholm," she said. "Come into the office."

They followed her into what had once been

a front parlour, now furnished only with a desk and computer, two chairs in front of the desk, and one behind it.

She waved a hand to indicate they should sit down and surveyed them with dark-brown suspicious eyes. "The nurse who originally looked after Mr. Harrison is one of our best, Harriet Macduff. Out of the blue, Mr. Harrison demanded Gloria Dainty. He said she was an old friend of the family and he had promised to keep an eye out for her. At that time, Gloria was nursing a Miss Whittaker and so Harriet took over her job and Gloria was sent to Mr. Harrison."

"And where can we find Miss Macduff?" asked Hamish.

"Number five, Tomintoul Brae, just outside the town on the Lairg road."

"What was your opinion of Gloria Dainty?" asked Hamish.

"She appeared to be a good nurse. She had been working at the hospital before deciding to go into private nursing. She seemed quiet and modest."

"Did she have any boyfriends?" asked Hamish.

"No one who called here, and we definitely do not encourage that sort of thing."

"Do you have a photo of her?" asked Charlie.

"There is a staff photo taken before she left to go to Mr. Harrison. Wait a minute."

Alexandra left the room. "Why do you want to see her photo?" asked Hamish. "I know what she looks like."

"Just an idea."

Alexandra came back. She held out a photograph. There were ten nurses in the photograph. "Which is Gloria?" asked Hamish, puzzled.

"Second from the left in the front row."

The Gloria in the photograph had brown hair. Like the other nurses, she was dressed in a dark-blue uniform with white collar and cuffs. She wore no make-up.

"May I take this?" asked Hamish. "I'll give you a receipt."

"Yes, if you think it will help you."

*   *   *

Outside, Hamish said, "You're a clever man, Charlie. Did you think she might have changed her appearance?"

"It crossed my mind. You said she looked like a fantasy nurse and I couldn't see that agency letting her go around dressed like that. I wondered suddenly if there might be a connection to Willie Dunne. Gloria wanted money. Maybe she hoped someone elderly might pop off and leave her some. She finds out which nurse is looking after which client and maybe finds out Harrison is the richest by getting Willie on the job."

"And," said Hamish excitedly, "all she had to do is wait until it's Harriet Macduff's day off, go up there all blonded and tarted up. Harrison agrees to tell the agency she's a friend o' the family. Let's go and see what Macduff has to say."

Miss Whittaker lived in a large sandstone house with a short drive leading up to it, bordered by rhododendron bushes.

There was a large garage to one side of the house and a small Ford Escort was parked outside it.

Hamish rang the bell. The door was opened by a tall woman in nurse's uniform. Hamish judged her to be in her fifties. She had a pleasant face and thick grey hair tied back.

"Miss Macduff?"

"Yes."

"Police. Sergeant Hamish Macbeth and Constable Carter. We would like to ask you some questions about Gloria Dainty."

"I barely knew the lassie. But come in. Be quiet because I've just got her down for her nap."

She led the way through to a kitchen. They all sat down at the table in the centre.

"Were you surprised when you were replaced by Gloria?" asked Hamish.

"Very surprised," she said. "Mr. Harrison and I got on just fine. When I protested, he was insulting and said he was tired of my ugly face. I was told to pack up and leave immediately. I was afraid I might have done something wrong.

I tried afterwards to phone Gloria several times, but it was always answered by Juris and he always said she was busy."

"Did you know her well?"

"No. I met her at the Christmas party. She seemed quiet, rather prim. The stuff that came out about her in the newspapers, you know, about her being blonde and beautiful amazed me."

"Did Miss Whittaker talk about her?"

"Not much. Oh, when I first arrived, she said, 'Don't expect any money in my will like that last one. I told her it all goes to my niece.'"

"Did she have any gentlemen callers?" asked Charlie.

She smiled. "What an old-fashioned laddie you are. Boyfriends? Maybe. Miss Whittaker told me she didn't want any men hanging around."

"I wish we could speak to her," said Hamish.

"Come back at four in the afternoon and I'll see what I can do."

As they were getting in the Land Rover, Hamish's phone rang so he switched it off.

"Switch off yours again as well, Charlie. It'll be Fiona wondering what the hell we're doing and I don't want to be taken away from here until we find out what Miss Whittaker has to say."

Hamish realised he was very hungry. He always seemed to be hungry these days. He had been so accustomed to Dick feeding him.

They found a café and ordered mutton pies, peas and chips, and a pot of tea.

"You were thinking," said Hamish, "that maybe Gloria had a boyfriend who put her up to it. She didn't have a criminal past. We never got to interview her sister, but I read the notes. Blameless background. And how would she know a sleazeball like Willie Dunne unless someone suggested him?"

"I think you'd better call the inspector," said Charlie, "or she may descend on the nursing agency looking for us and then go straight to Miss Whittaker's before we get a chance to talk to the old lady. If you tell her what we've got, she'll go straight to Harrison and ask why he didn't tell her about saying Gloria was a friend of the family."

"Maybe you're right, but thon one frightens me to death. I just hope it wasnae herself that burnt Willie to death."

"Don't be daft!" shouted Charlie. "She's an angel!"

"And a married one," said Hamish. "Oh, well, here goes."

Charlie listened dismally to the angry squawking coming down the phone, until Hamish interrupted, saying, "You must listen, ma'am. Charlie has had this brilliant idea."

Hamish talked rapidly and at length, finishing by telling her where they were and that they were waiting to interview Miss Whittaker. When he had finished, there was another brief squawk down the line before Hamish rang off.

"Don't worry, Charlie," he said. "She would ha' ordered us back if she didnae think we were on to something."

Fiona arrived at quarter to four and, with Hamish leading, followed them to Miss Whittaker's. Harriet said, "Miss Whittaker said she will be pleased to talk to you. She doesn't get many visitors. But be careful. She tires easily. She's ninety-three."

She led them up an oaken staircase and into a large bedroom. Miss Whittaker was seated in a chair by the window. She had dyed red hair and her old face was heavily made up. She was dressed in a long black velvet gown. Diamond rings sparkled on her thin hands, and a huge diamond-and-emerald brooch was pinned at the throat of her gown. Her faded-blue eyes were magnified by strong glasses.

Chairs had already been set up in a half circle in front of her. She waved an imperious hand for them to sit down.

Fiona switched on a tape recorder and began. "You are Miss Whittaker of number five, Tom-intoul Road, and—"

"For goodness' sakes!" snapped the old lady. "I am not a suspect and I am not under arrest. I don't like bossy women. Let that nice young man with the hair the same colour as my own ask any questions and switch off that stupid machine!"

Fiona gave a little shrug and nodded to

Hamish. "What did you make of Gloria Dainty?" asked Hamish.

"At first, she was fine. Very correct. Good at her job. Then the cracks began to appear."

"In what way?"

"Before I fell asleep, she would hold my hand and say things like, 'You must feel very lonely with no one but Gloria, who feels like your daughter.' Then once, when she thought I was asleep, I saw her taking a brooch out of my jewel box and trying it on. I shouted at her and she dropped it. She blushed and said she had only been admiring it. There have been various attempts during my long life to con money out of me. Once I heard a man's voice downstairs. I managed to drag myself to the landing and listened.

"'It's no use,' she was saying. 'We'll need to find someone else.'

"He said, 'I know someone. Hang on a bittie longer.' I rang the bell and when she came up I asked her who the man was. She said he was her brother. Two days later, she gave notice."

"She didn't have a brother," said Hamish.

"I think she and this man were looking for someone to prey on and found out about Mr. Harrison."

"Macbeth," ordered Fiona, "go and question the neighbours and see if you can get a description of this man."

"Go yourself, Miss Hoity-Toity," said the old lady. "I like talking to this young man."

"Oh, very well. Come along, Carter," said Fiona. No more Charlie, noted Hamish.

When they had left, Miss Whittaker rang the bell and told Harriet to bring tea and cakes. "Tell me all about it," she said to Hamish.

So Hamish told her about the case from the beginning, drinking tea and eating fruit cake while Fiona and Charlie waited impatiently outside.

When he had finished, she said, "So you think that Gloria and this man hoped I would take to her and leave her money in my will?"

"I think that might have been the case," said Hamish. "I think this man employed a seedy detective to find out some rich mark in the Highlands who needed a nurse."

"Will you come back and see me when you know more about it?" she asked.

"I certainly will. Now I had better join my boss. Before I leave, do you keep records of your phone bills?"

"I send everything to my accountant, Mr. Gerald Wither." She rang the bell and when Harriet came in asked her to fetch the accountant's address.

When Hamish emerged from the house, he saw Fiona and Charlie seated in the back of Fiona's car, their heads together, talking intently. He rapped on the window. Fiona looked up and scowled, and then she and Charlie got out of the car.

"You took your time," she said.

"I have the address of her accountant," said Hamish. "I thought it would be a good idea to go through her old phone bills. If Gloria phoned this man from the house, we might be able to find out who he is."

"I'll let you do that," said Fiona. "Charlie and I will go to headquarters to see if there is any further news about Andrew's alibi."

She and Charlie got back into her car, her driver let in the clutch, and they drove off.

So it's Charlie again, thought Hamish sadly. I wish she'd leave that innocent alone.

He looked at his watch. It was nearly five thirty. He got into his Land Rover and raced off, hoping to find the accountant still in his office.

Chapter Seven

*He's an Anglo-Saxon Messenger—and
those are Anglo-Saxon attitudes.*
                              —Lewis Carroll

Hamish caught Mr. Wither as the accountant
was just about to leave his office. He thought
that Wither was a good name for the bent little
old man. Surely he must be nearly as old as
Mrs. Whittaker.

He explained the reason for his visit and
Mr. Wither put his grey head on one side
like a bird searching for a worm. Then he
said in a high, thin voice, "My! This is very
exciting. Yes, I keep all the papers. Come
into the office. I am afraid my secretary has

left for the evening. Not that she would be much good. She has pictures of David Bowie painted on her nails and that seems to go along with lethargy and inefficiency. It's very hard to get good help these days when all the young want is to be famous without doing any work at all to get there."

Hamish stared in awe at the banks and banks of dusty files rising from floor to ceiling. "Don't you computerise this lot?"

"I wouldn't know where to start," he said ruefully. "I have an analog brain. But fear not. If you will just bring that ladder over."

"If you just point to what you want," said Hamish anxiously, "I'll get it for you."

"No, no. I'm quite spry." He scuttled up the ladder and pulled out a file. "Here we are. Whittaker. Phone bills. Catch!"

He threw the file down and Hamish caught it. "Have you a copying machine?" he asked.

"Oh, yes," said Mr. Wither proudly. He descended the ladder and went over to a corner of the office. He removed a pile of papers and said, "There it is."

"I'll just copy what I think are the relevant dates," said Hamish.

"Yes, yes, go ahead. Perhaps we might have a meal together when you are finished?"

Hamish turned round to refuse but was stopped short by the loneliness looking out of the old man's eyes. "Aye, that would be grand," he said.

The copying machine was so old that Hamish was relieved when it sprang into life.

After he had copies of all the bills he wanted, he switched off the machine and reluctantly followed Mr. Wither out of his office, wishing he didn't have to waste time going for dinner.

Mr. Wither led the way to a nearby restaurant called Scottish Fayre. It was in a converted haberdasher's. Hamish gloomily surveyed the menu. Why did they have to give everything silly descriptions? He settled for "Flora Macdonald's Cock-a-Leekie Soup," followed by "Over the Sea to Skye Cod and French Fries."

Mr. Wither said he would have the same and ordered a carafe of the house wine.

"Can't you get a decent secretary?" asked Hamish.

"I had Mrs. Richards for years and then she died. After that, I got temps from an agency. I advertise from time to time, but no one wants to work much in Strathbane. They prefer to register as unemployed and then work on the black."

"I might be able to help you out," said Hamish. "Mr. Patel runs the shop in Lochdubh and he's got a nephew here on a visit, a young lad who's a whiz wi' computers. I could send him over and you could see how you get on. He could computerise all your files and then give you lessons."

The old man gave a mischievous grin. "You are dragging me into the twenty-first century."

"Doesnae hurt," said Hamish.

Mr. Wither asked about the murders and Hamish told him all about them, and when dinner was over, he promised to return and give both Miss Whittaker and Mr. Wither the latest news.

When he got back to the police station, he phoned Mr. Patel and asked him if his nephew would be interested in working for Mr. Wither. "Jump at the chance," said Mr. Patel. "The laddie's bored out o' his skull."

Hamish then went into the office and studied the phone bills. There was a message from Fiona on his answering machine, demanding why he had not phoned to report progress. Hamish repressed a sigh. Such as the inspector would never understand Hamish's brand of policing, which was to help members of the public whenever possible.

He then settled down to check the phone numbers for the month preceding Gloria's murder.

He underlined five calls to a Strathbane number, picked up the phone, got through to the operator, and started the trace. He prayed the calls would not have come from a throwaway mobile. At last he was told the number belonged to an M. Hartford, 201 Bevan Mansions, in Strathbane.

Hamish was delayed from setting out by Lugs banging his food bowl on the floor and Sonsie trying to climb up him. He gave them tins of animal food and they both stared at him accusingly. "Oh, stop sulking," he said. "I'll get you fish-and-chips on the road home."

He felt uneasy on the drive to Strathbane. He should really inform police headquarters. Before he reached Strathbane, he pulled over to the side of the road and called Jimmy Anderson. It took some time to fill Jimmy in, but when he had finished, Jimmy said, "I'll meet you there. Let's hope this is our lad."

When Hamish drove up to Bevan Mansions, a seedy tower block down by the docks, it was to find not only Jimmy but also several police cars.

"If he looks out o' the window and sees this lot," complained Hamish, "he'll scarper."

"Stop bitching," said Jimmy, "and let's get on with it."

The lift didn't work and so they toiled up the filthy stairs. The walls were scarred with graffiti. Sounds of blaring television sets, crying children, and shouting voices assaulted their ears. "He's got form," said Jimmy.

"What for?"

"Drugs possession, carrying an offensive weapon, and drunk and disorderly. Malky Hartford. Lowlife."

"Whoever designed these flats should be shot," said Hamish, as they emerged onto the top-floor balcony. A biting wind blew discarded debris against their legs.

Jimmy knocked at Malky Hartford's door. Nothing but silence. Then the letterbox opened and two eyes stared out at them before closing it again.

"Police!" shouted Jimmy. "Open up!"

He put his ear to the door and heard scuffling sounds from inside. He signalled to a policeman behind them with a battering ram who moved forward and crashed the door open.

"There's a fire escape," shouted Hamish. He and Jimmy rushed through to the open window and looked out.

"Oh, my God!" yelled Jimmy. The rusting fire escape with Malky clinging to it had detached itself from the building. In the orange glare of the sodium streetlights below, they watched appalled as the whole huge fire escape swayed back and forth like some iron monster with Malky screaming and clinging to it, then went crashing down onto the roof of a disused warehouse opposite.

"No use rushing down," said Hamish. "There won't be much of him left." He could make out the crushed body of Malky under twisted pieces of rusty iron.

"I'll bag up that computer," said Jimmy. "And his mobile. I'll get the pathologist and the procurator out o' bed. We'll go back to the station and see if there's anything on the computer."

"Silly sod hasn't even encrypted the thing," said Jimmy at headquarters. "Let's get into his e-mail and see if we can find anything. By God! E-mails to none other than Gloria. Listen to this one, Hamish. 'I need a cut when you marry the old bugger. I paid Willie to find out the best mark. Didn't I tell you what to wear and how to get at him? Meet me down at the gates on Sunday...' We've got our man,

Hamish. The e-mail is dated for the night o' her murder."

"What else?"

" 'If you don't show, I'll let the polis know you was pinching drugs and flogging them through me.' "

"Go back to the earlier ones," said Hamish. "No, go to the in-box. Look, there's some from Gloria."

Jimmy read out: " 'I paid you in drugs, Malky, so consider yourself paid off and get out of my life. It was fun while it lasted, but I'm heading for the big time and I don't want you round my neck. Remember, I've got the goods on you and can shop you anytime I feel like it.' "

"No, she couldn't," said Hamish. "Not without Malky telling us about her."

"I 'member, Malky was pretty thick. He wouldnae think o' that."

"I wonder if she had a fling with him?"

"Could have," said Jimmy. "He was a good-looking fellow. Curly black hair and big blue eyes."

"If he's got family around," said Hamish,

"they'll be able to afford a grand funeral after they sue the council over that fire escape." He sighed wearily. "Let's print it all off. Check the mobile for texts and I'll let the inspector and Daviot know in the morning."

"I'll let them know, laddie," said Jimmy. "I'm your senior officer."

Hamish gave him a hurt look. "I'll give you credit," said Jimmy. "Honest."

"Then do the report yourself!" said Hamish furiously.

"No, no. Calm down. Start typing and explain what put you on to Malky."

A glaring red dawn was turning the frost on the heather to rubies as Hamish wearily drove back to Lochdubh. He let himself into the police station. Too tired to make breakfast, he went into his bedroom where his pets lay sleeping in his bed, tore off his uniform, crawled in beside them, and immediately fell asleep, down and down into a nightmare where Malky clung screaming to the disintegrating fire escape.

He was awakened five hours later by the sound of a large crash from the kitchen. He struggled out of bed and hurried through to find Charlie gazing miserably at a shattered milk jug on the floor.

"I'm right sorry, Hamish. I heard ye had a rough night so I thought I'd make you breakfast."

"It's all right," said Hamish, scrubbing the sleep from his eyes. "I never use that milk jug anyway. I aye just put the bottle on the table."

"I gather the case is solved," said Charlie. "Malky Hartford of all people."

Charlie stooped and shovelled up pieces of china into a dustpan, put them in the bin, and then mopped up the floor.

"I'll shower and shave," said Hamish, "and we'll talk about it. Where's the inspector?"

Charlie blushed. "Herself gone to consult wi' Daviot and the procurator fiscal and then she's off to Inverness."

Hamish eyed Charlie and thought, I hope he hasn't been seduced.

He washed and dressed and went back to

the kitchen, where Charlie was frying up a large pan of venison sausage. "I put a bit extra on for Lugs and Sonsie," said Charlie. "They're right partial to a bit o' venison. One egg or two?"

"Two, please."

"It's like the nightmare is over," said Charlie. "Mind you, I'd never ha' believed it o' Malky."

"You knew him?"

"Aye. A wee druggie. Do anything for a fix. But a handsome lad for all that. But murdering people! I cannae believe that. Now it turns out that lassie up in Kinlochbervie was poisoned wi' antifreeze. That's a slow, vicious death. Still, drugs can change folks' characters. Just as well for Andrew and his missus. They werenae in Somerset."

Hamish sat down at the table. "Where were they?"

"In Edinburgh."

"What were they doing?"

"It's a high-class wife-swopping club. Most of them English."

"Crivens!" said Hamish, a picture of Andrew's angular wife appearing in his mind. "Talk about Anglo-Saxon attitudes!"

"The inspector was going to charge both of them wi' perverting the course of justice, or defeating the ends of justice as we say in Scotland, when she got the news that the murders were solved. She was so delighted that she let them off with a caution."

Charlie put four sausages and two eggs on a plate and put it on the table along with a pot of tea.

"I cannae believe it's all over. Did you and herself celebrate?"

Charlie bent over to put sausages into the animals' bowls. "No time for that," he mumbled.

I do believe they've been and gone and done it, thought Hamish. Damn the woman. What now? Will she get a divorce? Will I lose this decent copper who suits me just fine?

Instead, he said, "I put my report in. Do they want anything more from me?"

"I shouldnae think so," said Charlie, easing his great height down onto a kitchen chair and helping himself to tea. "Daviot is holding a press conference and taking all the credit, no doubt. If you don't want me for anything today, I thought maybe me and George, I mean the colonel, might take the rods out."

"Fishing season's over, Charlie."

"I meant, take the boat out and maybe get some fresh mackerel."

"Go ahead. I'll eat this and take Sonsie and Lugs for a walk. It looks like a grand day."

When he walked along the waterfront, dressed in comfortable old clothes, having decided to give himself the day off, Hamish looked at the little white houses of the village and wondered why he could not experience any feeling of relief.

He saw the Currie sisters approaching. Had he not had the dog and cat with him, he would probably have jumped over the wall onto the beach to escape them. He always thought of the spinster twins as the Greek chorus of Lochdubh. Doom and gloom from the pair of them.

"I see that clever Mr. Daviot solved the case for you," said Nessie.

"Solved," intoned her sister.

"It is just as well someone was on the job and not lazing around with a dog and cat," said Nessie.

"Dog and cat," moaned her sister.

"Oh, shove off, the pair of you," said Hamish. They stared up at him, shocked eyes behind thick spectacles, rigidly permed white hair, and crumpled white faces, the skin like tissue paper.

They marched off.

"Sorry!" shouted Hamish after them. "I'm so sorry."

He scratched his fiery hair in distress. What had come over him?

He saw the fisherman Archie Maclean sitting on the wall outside his little cottage at the harbour and went to join him.

"I'm going daft," said Hamish. "I've just insulted the Currie sisters."

"They'll get over it," said Archie. "I hear those murders have been solved."

"Yes, it's all over," said Hamish. But he experienced the first sharp pang of doubt.

"You'd better settle down now and find your-self a wifie," said Archie.

"I'm beginning to think I have no luck at all in that direction," said Hamish.

Archie deftly rolled up a cigarette, shoved it in his toothless mouth, lit it, and said, "You should ask the fairies."

"You don't believe in that rubbish, do you, Archie?"

"All you do," said Archie, "is put out a bit o' milk, salt, and iron outside your door and wait."

"You're joshing. I'm off to get some weight off these beasties o' mine."

When Hamish returned to the police station, he saw with a mixture of irritation and amuse-ment that outside the kitchen door Archie had placed a small saucer of milk, a little open glass jar of salt, and a piece of iron.

Well, thought Hamish with a shrug, if I had a wife like Archie's, I'd need to believe in some-thing daft to keep me going. Archie's wife was a fanatical housecleaner. She boiled all the house-hold laundry in an old-fashioned copper, including Archie's trousers and jackets—which explained why the fisherman always went around in tight clothes.

He passed the day cleaning up the police station and giving his small flock of sheep winter feed.

He walked the dog and cat again, wondering whether to call on the Currie sisters and apologise, but found himself unable to face up to it.

When Hamish walked back into the police station, he experienced a sharp pang of loneliness. There was no point in going to join Charlie, because the big policeman would be settling down for a family evening with the colonel and his wife.

Sonsie came up and put a large paw on his knee. "You don't believe in the fairies, do you, Sonsie? Load o' superstitious rubbish!"

There came a sharp scream of rising wind which rattled the kitchen door. Hamish stood, startled.

Then the door opened and Elspeth Grant walked in. "It's me," she said. "You look as if you've seen a ghost."

"I'm fine. Sit down. Windy out?"

"No, it's as still as the grave. Going to be a sharp frost. I've just been down to Strathbane. Boring footage of Daviot. I suppose you broke the case."

"In a way."

"So it's all over?"

"I suppose. We'll never know. I am sure that Malky's family will sue the socks off the council."

"I've tried to interview the provost, but he's hiding behind his lawyer and everyone else in the council has been taught to say, 'No comment.'"

Elspeth was wearing a silver puffa jacket that matched the colour of her odd eyes. She shrugged it off. Underneath she was wearing a blue cashmere sweater. She had small, high, firm breasts.

"I've got a bottle of Hungarian champagne out in the shed," said Hamish. "We could have a glass to celebrate."

"Bring it on, just so long as it doesn't have any antifreeze in it."

"That was Austria," said Hamish, referring to an old scandal.

He went out to the shed. The champagne had been a present from a grateful woman after Hamish had tracked down her lost dog. Antifreeze, he thought suddenly. That's what killed Jessie McGowan. Now, why would someone like Malky get to hear about her? And even if he had, would Malky, a druggie and city boy, believe in anyone being able to have the second sight? Even if he did, the second sight meant the future.

Elspeth appeared behind him, making him jump. "I thought you'd got lost," she said.

"No. Just thinking. It's right cold. Let's get indoors."

On the way in, Elspeth glanced down at the milk, salt, and iron. "Didn't know you were a believer, Hamish."

"I'm not. It is just Archie's nonsense."

She gave a sudden shiver. "Now, why do I suddenly feel you are soon going to need a lot of protection?"

Hamish looked down at her uneasily. He knew from past experience that Elspeth, who came from a Gypsy family, was psychic.

He lifted two wineglasses down from the cupboard. "I havenae got champagne flutes. These'll need to do."

"There's been a recent report that flutes are out of fashion," said Elspeth. "Something to do with them spoiling the taste."

Hamish popped the cork and filled two glasses.

"Here's to a quiet life," he said.

"Here's to your safety," said Elspeth. "So let's have it, Hamish. You don't think Malky did the murders. How did that detective die?"

"Willie? The latest was smoke inhalation. Now, that could have been Malky. He was in cahoots wi' Gloria. He may not have known that Willie would be in the office. It was a Sunday morning. I had an appointment with him."

"How was the fire started?"

"Oily flaming rags shoved through the letter box. That might indeed have been Malky. But there's another thing."

He told Elspeth about Willie spying on Fiona. "I'm sure that could have been Blair. The inspector is keen on Charlie, and it shows."

"Blair's a monster," said Elspeth, "but I can't believe he would murder Willie."

"He may not have known he was in the office."

"If I were you," said Elspeth, "I would take time out and forget about the whole thing and clear your mind of every idea. Maybe then you'd hit on something."

Elspeth then began to talk about her job and her seemingly eternal fears of being replaced permanently by another presenter while she was off in the Highlands reporting until they re-alised with surprise that they had finished the bottle of champagne.

If only, thought Hamish wistfully, we could roll into bed and make love for the rest of the day. But as if she had read his mind, Elspeth put on her coat and said abruptly, "Thanks for the drink."

"Will I see you again this trip?"

"No, I'm heading off south," said Elspeth.

As she walked to the car she had borrowed from the hotel, not wanting to take the large television van down to the police station, she had a sudden urge to turn back. She had lied to

Hamish. She had planned to prepare her report and leave on the following morning. She could have invited Hamish to dinner.

Hamish was leaving the police station to walk the dog and cat. He looked down in disgust at Archie's offerings to the fairies and gave the lot a kick with his regulation boot and sent them flying.

Elspeth had half turned back when a voice in her head said, Going to get hurt again?

She squared her shoulders, got into the car, and drove off.

As he walked along, Hamish saw a sign outside the church hall, TAI CHI EXERCISES.

A faint sound of Asian music tinkled through the frosty air. Curious, he walked up to the village hall and quietly pushed open the door. Eight village women, dressed in sort of satin pyjamas, were slowly following movements by an instructor, who, Hamish realised, was none other than Mrs. Wellington. He had seen tai chi exercises on television and they had been nothing like this. The women seemed to be all sharp, awkward movements.

"The hell wi' this," said Mrs. Patel, sitting down suddenly on the floor. "I feel right daft."

The other women followed suit. "Now, ladies," boomed Mrs. Wellington in distress. "On your feet. Now!"

Muttering rebelliously, they started again. Hamish fled the church hall and hung on to the fence, laughing. He felt better than he had done for a long time.

When he returned to the police station, he saw Charlie's old Volvo parked outside. The tall policeman got out of the car when he saw Hamish arriving.

"I should ha' reported in earlier," said Charlie, "but I overslept."

There was a miserable hangdog air about him.

"Come in and have coffee," said Hamish. "No, better still. Let's walk along to the Italian's and have a wee celebration. I suppose the case is closed."

They walked in silence to the restaurant. Inside, Lugs and Sonsie vanished into the kitchen.

"Now," said Hamish when they had placed their orders. "Out wi' it."

"Out wi' what?" demanded Charlie mutinously.

"You look miserable and guilty as sin. Is it our inspector? I thought she'd cleared off."

Charlie stabbed his fork into the new tablecloth. "Here!" screeched the waiter, Willie Lamont. "Thon's a new cloth. You're a right wondle."

"I suppose you mean vandal," said Hamish. "Shove off and get the food."

When Willie had gone, Hamish said gently, "What has she done?"

Charlie heaved a great sigh. "Do you believe in hell?"

"Of course not."

"I was brought up Wee Free," said Charlie, meaning the Free Presbyterians. "A woman taken in adultery is a sin."

"Damn the woman!" said Hamish. "She seduced you."

"Well, Hamish, it takes two. Aye, we spent the night together. I told her I loved her and I would make an honest woman of her and she laughed her head off and said it was only a fling."

"Here's the wine. Have a glass. It's my belief you were more sinned against than sinning."

"I felt such a rage, I damn nearly broke her neck. Oh, I'm so ashamed. Will God forgive me?"

"Look, Charlie, I cannae believe in a God who punishes or even rewards because they are both human failings. Forget it. Put it down to experience. Were you a virgin?"

Charlie shook his head. "Just the odd widow here and there."

"Not here I hope," said Hamish sharply. "Don't shit on your own doorstep."

"No, no, I promise you that."

"Look, after we eat, we'll go to the manse and you tell the minister about it. He's a genuine Christian and you need one o' those. Then I'd like to go down to Strathbane on the quiet and see if I can talk to people who knew Malky. There's something nagging me. Okay, Andrew and his wife were at some wife-swopping party in Edinburgh. One of them could have slipped out and driven north. Anyway, it would make me feel easier. We won't wear our uniforms and we'll take your car."

*   *   *

After lunch, they left the animals at the station and walked up to the manse. To Hamish's relief, there was no sign of Mrs. Wellington.

Mr. Wellington led them into his dark and gloomy study. "Charlie here needs help," said Hamish.

The minister listened carefully as Charlie blurted out his story. When Charlie had finished, Mr. Wellington said, "I have seen the inspector. She is a much older woman, is she not?"

Charlie nodded.

"Married?"

He nodded again.

"You have been preyed upon by an older, experienced woman," said Mr. Wellington. "You must ask the Lord to heal your hurt. But the fault lies with her. There are plenty of bonny lassies in the Highlands, and I suggest you find one. What do you feel now?"

"I feel like you do when you've been drinking too much the night afore," said Charlie, "and you wake up feeling dirty and smelly."

"That's good. A broken heart is a more difficult matter. Is your heart broken?"

Muddled thoughts like cloud shadows chased across Charlie's face. "I think it's all right, sir."

"Grand. Be more careful next time. There are harpies around. Not," added the minister wistfully, "that I have ever met one."

The door crashed open and Mrs. Wellington appeared. "What is going on here?"

"Charlie here is Wee Free," said Hamish, "but he's thinking o' changing to the Church of Scotland. Come along, Charlie."

Outside, Charlie said, "That man's a saint."

"He'd have to be, married to a wife like that," said Hamish.

Chapter Eight

O, wally, wally, gin love be bonnie
A little time while it is new!
But when 'tis auld it waxeth cauld
And fades awa' like morning dew.

—Scottish ballad

But when they arrived at the tower block, it was to find the area swarming with council officials.

"We can't hang around here," said Hamish, "or we'll be caught by someone from Strathbane. I know a café where the druggies hang out."

The sky above had darkened and a little hard flake of snow drifted down, followed by another.

By the time they entered the café, a full blizzard
was blowing outside. Hamish looked around.
"See anyone from your days down here?" he
asked.

"Aye, over in the corner," said Charlie. "Jonty
Hill. Used to give me wee bits o' information."
They collected cups of tea from the counter
and joined Jonty, who squinted up at them nervously. He was an ill-favoured youth with a
pasty face and greasy hair. He was huddled into
a stained donkey jacket. "It's yourself, Charlie."

"What can you tell us about Malky?" asked
Charlie. He took out a twenty-pound note and
rolled it in his fingers.

Jonty eyed it greedily. "Malky was a right nice
wee guy. All this talk about him being some
sort of serial killer is havers. Wouldnae even kill
a cockroach."

"I think he might have burned Willie Dunne
to death," said Hamish.

"If he set fire to thon office, it would be because he thought there was no one inside."

"What relatives does he have?"

"It was on the telly this morning. His ma

is suing the council. 'Her darling boy,' and all that. She chucked him out three years ago."

"Did Malky have a girlfriend?" asked Hamish.

"They were more druggies in arms," said Jonty. He seemed to think he had made a very witty remark because he doubled up with laughter which ended in a wheezing cough.

"Where does she live and what's her name?" asked Charlie.

"Gemma Burns. There's an auld house out on the Lairg road. Called Brae House. It's a squat."

Charlie passed over the note. "Try spending that on food, Jonty."

"Aye, sure, man. I'm clean."

Hamish and Charlie hurried through the blizzard to Charlie's car. "It's a good thing the heater still works in this old bus and I got the snow tyres put on last week," said Charlie. "Do you think we should try to make it back to Lochdubh? I don't want to be stuck down here in this hellhole."

"Oh, let's get it over with," said Hamish. "It may stop snowing. What was the weather forecast?"

"Snow flurries."

"I don't think those weather folk ever look out the damn window. Look, there's a gritter up ahead on the Lairg road. That'll make the going easier."

"I remember where this Brae House is," said Charlie. "When I was working down here, we had to evict a lot o' druggies. The owner went bankrupt and it was claimed by the bank, but by that time it was such a ruin, no one wanted to buy the place."

They moved forward through the white world in silence, until at last Charlie said, "There's the place. Up on the left. And there's smoke coming from one o' the chimneys."

They drove up the short drive and parked outside.

"Don't knock," ordered Hamish as they got out. "If the door's open, just walk in."

The door was unlocked. They walked into a square hall and were hit by a foul smell caused by bad drains, unwashed bodies, old food, and a fresh smell of pot.

Following the smell of hashish, Hamish opened a door on the left of the hall. Three miserable specimens of humanity were huddled round the fireplace. A young man who had been about to pass the roach in his fingers to a girl next to him threw it in the fire.

"You're cops," accused a young girl with so many piercings on her face that Hamish wondered if the metal was a good idea in such a freezing winter. Surely it added to the misery.

"We're not here about drugs, nor are we here to evict you," said Hamish. "Did any of you know Malky? Is Gemma Burns here?"

There was a silence. Then, "That's me," said the girl with the piercings. Another long silence. Snow pattered against a cracked window and wind howled in the chimney. Then a youth with a large black beard and a bald head said, "I kent Malky. He wasnae a murderer."

"What makes you say that?" asked Charlie.

"Well, he'd steal a bit, maybe, for the drugs. But kill anyone? I cannae believe it."

Charlie was about to ask for his name, but a warning look from Hamish, whose highland radar had immediately known what he was about to ask, stopped him. Hamish only wanted to hear about Malky and didn't want this source of information to dry up.

"Did he have a girlfriend?" asked Hamish. "I mean, other than Gemma?"

"He said he had a posh lassie who gave him drugs, methadone and stuff. He said she was a right cracker and had a scam that would see him all right."

"Did you ever see her?"

He shook his head.

"But what makes you think he couldn't murder anyone?" pursued Hamish. "If Malky was into hard drugs, then his brain could have been twisted and fried."

Gemma piped up. "Well, he couldn't have murdered thon nurse."

"What makes you say that?"

"Because from the night she disappeared

until her body was found, Malky was here wi'
us, chilling out."

Hamish stared at them, his brain whirling. If
he took them in and got their statements, the
fury of Daviot would know no bounds. Daviot
had gloried in the "solution" to the murders.
He, Hamish, would be suspended for going out
on his own on Strathbane's patch.

The inspector, he thought. Fiona Herring, he
knew, would be intrigued. He was furious with
her for having seduced Charlie, but he knew her
to be a good officer.

Another girl said, "Will we have to leave here?"

"I'd like to suggest you all check into a clinic
and get off drugs," said Hamish. "I'll keep quiet
about it until I figure out what to do."

When he and Charlie were outside, Hamish
said, "If we take them in, they won't be listened
to. Daviot wants the case kept closed. I'll be
cursed for dragging in three filthy druggies who
probably don't know the day of the week. Charlie, I'm going to see the inspector when this
blizzard blows over."

"I never want to see that woman again," howled Charlie.

"I'll deal with her."

Unlike the busier parts of Scotland, the roads of the Highlands were usually kept clear with gritters and snow ploughs. As they reached Lochdubh, the snow stopped and the clouds parted.

"You go to the hotel," said Hamish. "I'll let you know what happens."

"You'll want this," said Charlie, handing him a small tape recorder. "I taped the whole thing."

"Man, you're a genius. Off you go."

Hamish went into the police station and collected the dog and cat while he went up to check on his sheep. Returning to the police station, he began the job of getting snowballs out of their coats before feeding them.

Then he put on his uniform and set out for Inverness.

Christmas lights sparkled in the windows of shops when he drove into Inverness. The whole place looked like a Christmas card. He suddenly wished he had phoned first. What if Fiona were down in Edinburgh with her husband?

With a sinking heart, he learned that Fiona was off duty. He asked if his friend Mungo Davidson was on duty, found to his relief that he was, and asked to see him.

"Why do you want to contact Old Iron Knickers?" asked Mungo.

"It's too long a story. Do you know where she lives?"

"I know where she is at the moment. Her ladyship is out wi' her husband for dinner. They're at the Taste Of France restaurant in the High Street."

"Let me use the phone in your office. I'll call her."

Fiona, when she came to the phone, appeared to be furious that her caller was none other than Hamish Macbeth. "What the hell do you think you are doing, interrupting my evening off?" she raged.

"Listen!" said Hamish urgently. He began to tell her rapidly and concisely what they had learned about Malky. When he had finished, she said, "Get back to your station and I will call on you in the morning."

Mungo, who had left his office while Hamish was phoning, met him on the road out. "Flea in both ears?" he asked sympathetically.

"Something like that," said Hamish, and hurried off.

In the morning, he awoke early, showered, and put on his uniform. He reluctantly allowed the dog and cat out to play. He walked to Patel's and bought the morning paper. He was relieved to learn that the wild cat sanctuary of about five hundred square miles at Ardnamurchan was being extended to Morven. I hope the beasties breed and breed, he thought, so that there'll be so many wild cats no one will bother about Sonsie.

He heard a knock at the kitchen door. He reluctantly went to open it, hoping that his dislike for the inspector would not show. Why couldn't the wretched woman have left Charlie alone?

But it was Charlie who came lumbering in. "Maybe I should send you away on something," said Hamish.

"I'll probably have to see her sometime," said Charlie. "I've brought you a tray o' shortbread from the chef, some bones for Lugs, and a fish for Sonsie."

"I'll phone him later and thank him. Coffee?"

"Grand."

Hamish turned and put the kettle on the stove. "Where is that bloody woman?" he said.

"Here," said a voice from the kitchen door. Fiona had walked in quietly. Her eyes, hard and mean, fell on Sonsie. The cat was lying by the stove.

"That *is* a wild cat," she said. "And I feel it my duty to report it."

Hamish's hazel eyes blazed, but before he could say anything, Charlie commented, "It's just a big pussycat. It would be a shame to take up police time with a false report—like some of the reports of sexual harassment."

Fiona glared at him. Unfazed, Charlie smiled back.

She pulled out a chair and sat down. "What's all this about?" she demanded.

"Just what I told you on the phone, ma'am," said Hamish. "Would you like some coffee?"

"No! Oh, well yes."

Hamish reached into the cupboard for cups and said over his shoulder, "Play the tape for the inspector, Charlie."

She listened intently. When it was finished, she said, "Why didn't you arrest them?"

"And let Strathbane know we'd been poaching on their patch? It is my belief that Mr. Daviot would be so furious, he would discount the whole thing. He would say that druggies would say anything and they never knew what day it was. Then there is the alibi of Andrew Harrison. He claims that he and his wife were at a wife-swopping party in Edinburgh. Now why say that? He could just have claimed to have been at an ordinary party and I'm sure the other people there would ha' backed him up. They must all be furious with him. So if by any chance he or his wife could have slipped out at any time, I'm sure they would tell us."

He put a mug of coffee and a plate of short-bread down in front of her.

She drank coffee and ate a finger of short-bread. Hamish and Charlie waited in silence.

"I tell you what I'll do," she said at last. "I will handle the Edinburgh end. You go about your normal duties and wait to hear from me."

"Yes, ma'am," said Hamish, thinking he would be glad of a day off. He waited un-easily, praying she would not ask Charlie to accompany her, but she rose, nodded to them, and walked out.

There was a long silence. Then Hamish asked, "How do you feel, Charlie?"

He looked puzzled. "I don't feel anything. It's like having a bad fall and then finding nothing's broken. Is the snow still deep?"

"Pretty deep," said Hamish, "and no sign of a thaw. I was hoping we might have a day off, but we'd better check up on the old people and see they're all right."

*   *   *

After a long and tiring day, Hamish said, "I never want to see another cup of tea again." At each place they had visited on their enormous beat, highland hospitality demanded they accept refreshment.

Charlie said he would go back to the hotel. He was welcomed by the colonel. "Just in time to join us for dinner, Charlie. Priscilla is back on one of her flying visits."

Charlie hesitated. "All right. But I'll just have a salad or something. I'm up to the eyeballs in tea and scones. Been out wi' Hamish, checking on the old folk. I'll just change out of my uniform."

"No need for that," said the colonel. "You're one of the family."

Charlie was once more taken aback by the beauty that was Priscilla. From the perfect bell of her golden hair to her slim figure dressed in a mid-blue trouser suit that matched her eyes, he thought she looked stunning.

"You're busy," said Charlie, looking round the crowded dining room.

"I hope I haven't made a mistake," said Priscilla. "There's probably going to be a sighting of the northern lights this evening, so I put it on the website and people came rushing up. If nothing happens, I hope they don't ask for their money back."

Charlie suddenly noticed that Priscilla was wearing an engagement ring. "It looks as if congratulations are in order," he said. "Who's the lucky fellow?"

"Probably another waste of space," muttered her father.

"It's an old friend of the family," said Mrs. Halburton-Smythe. "Harold Fox-Enderby."

"He's too old," growled the colonel.

"Can I get a word in here?" demanded Priscilla. "He'll be joining us soon, Charlie. I met him in London. He's a stockbroker for a firm I used to do computer work for."

I wonder how Hamish will take this news, thought Charlie. I wonder if he ever really got over her.

The dining room began to clear, and soon

huddled-up figures appeared on the terrace outside the long windows.

"I hope I haven't made a terrible mistake," said Priscilla.

"About your engagement?" asked Charlie.

"No, of course not! I meant the aurora borealis. I wish now I had employed some technician from the film industry to fake it for me."

Suddenly there was a great cheer from the terrace, the waiters switched off the lights in the dining room, and the great, swirling spectacle of the northern lights filled the room with greenish light.

"Hullo there!" called a voice. Charlie looked up. A burly middle-aged man was bending over to kiss Priscilla on the cheek.

"Harold," said Priscilla, "meet my parents. And Charlie Carter, a friend of the family."

What on earth does she see in him? marvelled Charlie. He's too old for her.

Harold had a sallow, pugnacious face with designer stubble. He had small eyes and a fleshy nose and large thick lips. His shirt was open at the neck, displaying tufts of hair.

"What's all this?" he asked. "Son et lumière?"

"No, it's the aurora borealis," said Charlie.

"Can we get you something to eat?" asked the colonel.

"No, I had something on the road up. I'll have a coffee." He sat down next to Priscilla and put an arm around her shoulders.

"And how is your dear mother?" asked Mrs. Halburton-Smythe.

"Lost her wits. She's in a home."

"Oh, dear. Poor Bertha. How awful."

"Happens to all of us, some time or another," said Harold. "Mind you, the home costs a mint. Daylight robbery. I can see my inheritance going down the tubes with every day that passes."

"Is your father dead?" asked Charlie.

"Yes, broke his neck on the hunting field ten years ago. What a godforsaken part of the country this is. Miles and miles of nothingness."

The lights came on again in the dining room. But it was as if a shadow had crossed Priscilla's face. "You'll see more of it tomorrow," she said. "It is very beautiful."

Charlie stifled a yawn. "If you folk will forgive me, I've had a hard day and I'd like to get to bed."

The colonel rose to his feet. "I'll see you downstairs, Charlie."

No sooner were they in Charlie's flat than the colonel started. "Why did she choose that ape? He's been married before."

"Divorce?"

"No, fell downstairs and broke her neck. I bet he pushed her," said the colonel viciously. "I've never believed psychiatrists to be any good, but I wish now I'd sent her to one after that episode."

"What episode?" asked Charlie.

"Never mind. Long time ago. What about a dram?"

"I'll make up the fire," said Charlie.

"Don't need to. The central heating works down here."

"George, I like a fire," said Charlie stubbornly. The fire was set and ready to light. He struck a match, lit it, and then got out a bottle of whisky and two glasses.

The colonel settled back in an armchair. "Would you like to earn a bit o' money, Charlie?"

"If you want me to do something for you, I'll do it for nothing," said Charlie.

"This is serious stuff. I want you to get rid of Harold."

"Kill him?"

"No, no. Cut him out with Priscilla. You're a good-looking fellow. Pitch in there!"

"How long is your daughter up here for?" asked Charlie.

"Just a couple of days."

"Even if I wanted to, I couldnae romance any lassie in two days. Priscilla has been engaged before and I don't mean just to Hamish."

"Never came to anything."

"So," said Charlie, "I'll bet you this one will fizzle out."

"But there were nasty rumours about Harold when he was married. Said he beat his wife."

Charlie sat, nursing his glass of whisky and looking into the leaping flames of the fire. At last he said, "I have this chap I went to school with, Lochy Cullen. He was christened Lochinver by his ma who was a fan o' Walter Scott. That got him picked on in school. I beat off his tormentors because he was a puny wee chap. But I couldnae be there for him all the time. When he got to his teens, he shot up in height and started bodybuilding, and then he began to punch everyone who had tormented him. He works as a bouncer at a posh club in London. Now, here's an idea. You could pay him to keep an eye on Priscilla. Maybe just for the next fortnight. He might be glad o' a break from the club. He phones me from time to time. Have you got keys to Priscilla's flat in London?"

"Yes, me and the wife stay there when we're in London. Why?"

"Just in case Lochy hears noises of violence and has to burst in."

"Phone him now!"

"Right. I may get him at the club. You go upstairs. Leave your watch behind. If I come up and hand it to you, you'll know everything's been set up. Now, to the money business."

The colonel came up with a generous sum, left Charlie, and went reluctantly back to the dining room. His wife was sitting alone with Priscilla. "Where's Harold?" asked the colonel.

"The poor lamb was tired and he's gone to bed," said Priscilla.

Lamb, thought the colonel furiously. More like wolf in sheep's clothing. Priscilla began to talk about hotel business while the colonel only half listened until he heard, with relief, Charlie's voice saying, "You left your watch."

"Thanks, Charlie. Thanks a lot!"

Charlie reported to the police station in the morning and Hamish listened in dismay to his news. When he had finished, Hamish said, "I got a call from the inspector. She's still working on Andrew's alibi. Probably be back up here tomorrow if she gets a breakthrough. We'd better get up to the hotel and see her while she's here. I'll see if Angela will look in on Sonsie and Lugs."

Angela said she didn't mind as long as the animals were left in the police station and not in her home, frightening her cats. Hamish and Charlie set out for the hotel. They called on the manager, Mr. Johnson, first of all and explained the problem. He said he would alert the staff to keep an eye on Priscilla. "But right now they've gone out for a run," said the manager.

"Damn! We'd better search for them," said Hamish. "Any idea where they went?"

"I think Priscilla said something about going to visit Dick and Anka."

"Right. We'd better get over there."

In Braikie, they headed up the side stairs to the flat above, knowing that Dick and Anka would be doing business online while staff served in the shop.

They paused outside the door and listened. They could clearly hear Harold saying, "What is a divine creature like you doing living in a dump like this? I could get you a job in London as a model. I also know people in the television and film industry."

Enough, thought Hamish, and he opened the

door. Four faces turned to look at them. Priscilla's was a frozen mask. Dick looked furious. Harold was plainly leering at Anka, and Anka greeted them with patent relief.

"Come in, Hamish and Charlie. We are so glad to see you."

"I am afraid we are just leaving," said Priscilla. "Come along, Harold."

He gave her a baffled look but followed her out. "Tell you later," said Hamish. "Got to follow them."

He hurried down the stairs and peered round into the street. Harold and Priscilla were getting into Harold's Range Rover. As it started up, Hamish noticed with delight that one of the brake lights wasn't working.

"His brake light's out," he said to Charlie. "Let's stop them. Tell you what. You go to Braikie garage and tell Jake there's fifty pounds for him if he finds something else wrong or makes something else wrong."

Hamish jumped in his Land Rover and with siren wailing and blue light flashing, he set off in pursuit. Harold pulled to the side of the road. Hamish got out and rapped on the driver's window. When Harold lowered it, Hamish said, "You have a broken brake light and you cannot proceed unless you get it fixed."

"Do we need to do it now, Hamish?" asked Priscilla. "It's just a minor thing."

Hamish ignored her and said to Harold, "There's the garage a few yards back. Take your vehicle there."

Muttering about highland peasants, Harold turned his car around and headed for the garage.

Charlie saw him coming and quickly moved out of the garage and went to join Hamish.

"That'll keep the scunner busy for a while," said Hamish. "Let's go to the pub for lunch."

But when they emerged an hour later and strolled to the garage it was to find that Harold and Priscilla had gone.

"What went wrong?" demanded Hamish.

"I tried my best," said Jake. "But thon fellow knew as much about cars as me. Here's your fifty back."

"Any idea where they went?" asked Hamish.

"I told them the Falls of Shin over by Lairg would look right pretty in the snow."

"We'll try there," said Hamish.

By the Falls of Shin, Harold shouted above the roar of the water, "Are we going to stand here freezing all day? Think of it, Priscilla. We could be in London, instead of freezing our arses up here. Mind you, I know a good way to keep warm." He jerked her into his arms and forced his mouth down on hers. Priscilla began to struggle. "Not here," she pleaded, jerking her mouth back. He abruptly released her and then swore. A snowball had struck him on the back of the head.

He looked wildly around. "Where did that come from?"

"Probably kids," said Priscilla. "We'll go back to the car and find somewhere to eat."

They climbed back up to the car park. That was when Harold found that his car would not start. Cursing, he got out and lifted the bonnet. "The distributor leads have gone!" he yelled.

He looked up at the sound of an approaching

vehicle to see the police Land Rover turning into the car park.

Hamish Macbeth climbed down and approached them. "Oh, it is yourselves," he said. "Some wee laddies phoned up and said a woman was being raped down at the falls."

"You can help out," snarled Harold. "Someone has stolen the distributor leads."

"I'll get someone from the nearest garage over. It'll be quicker than phoning the Automobile Association. We'll take Priscilla with us because it's too cold for a lady to wait here."

"I'll come, too," said Harold.

"Och, no need for that," said Hamish. "What if the thief came back and took the whole car?"

"It's all right, Harold," said Priscilla. "I won't be long."

Charlie moved into the back and Priscilla climbed into the passenger seat. "Now," she said angrily, "did you stage this?"

"Why would I do that?" asked Hamish.

"To spoil my fun."

"Oh, my." Hamish threw on the brakes. "I

should ha' known you'd prefer to be wi' your fiancé."

"Just drive on!" snapped Priscilla.

The garage in Lairg was closed for DINNER, as the notice on the door said, dinner still being served in the middle of the day. They found out that the garage owner lived in a bungalow down by the loch, but he refused to move until he had finished his dinner of barley soup, stew, and apple crumble. Priscilla tried to phone Harold but could not get a reply. The reason was that Harold was sure Hamish had planned the whole thing. Thirsting for revenge, he phoned police headquarters in Strathbane and said he wished to report Sergeant Hamish Macbeth, who had deliberately sabotaged his car.

Blair heard of the call and said he would deal with it. This, he was sure, was Hamish trying to cover up something sinister. For Hamish had not put in a report. Careless of expense, he commandeered the police helicopter and set off.

Harold heard the whir of the helicopter overhead and got out of his car. The helicopter descended, covering him in a small blizzard. Blair and two policemen got out.

"Come with us," ordered Blair. "We'll sort this out at headquarters."

"I am not going anywhere, you stupid moron," raged the snowman that was Harold. "This is like the Keystone Cops."

"Handcuff him," ordered Blair. "I am charging you with abusing a senior police officer."

Hamish, Priscilla, and Charlie looked up in the sky and saw the helicopter lifting off. "I think that was ower at the falls," said Charlie.

"Probably some poor soul has had a heart attack or something," said Hamish. "We'd better get to his car and fix it."

He raced ahead of the mechanic. "You stay in the car, Priscilla," said Hamish. "Don't want you getting cold."

He quickly replaced the distributor leads before the mechanic arrived. But Harold had taken the car keys with him. Hamish looked around and then down at the blown circle of snow. "He must have had an accident," he said. "That helicopter must have been for Harold."

He phoned the Air Ambulance, but they said they had not picked anyone up from Lairg.

Detective Chief Inspector Blair was a very un-lucky man. Daviot was leaving the police station just as a handcuffed Harold was being marched inside.

"I wish to use my phone," Harold was shouting. "My fiancée, Priscilla Halburton-Smythe, will wonder what has happened to me."

"May I be of assistance?" asked Daviot.

Harold burst out with the whole story.

Daviot's pale eyes fastened on Blair. "Why is this gentleman in handcuffs?"

"He insulted me," said Blair.

"What exactly did he say?"

"He said that Macbeth had sabotaged his car."

"Did you phone Macbeth and demand an ex-planation?"

"It seemed too important to wait. So I took the helicopter up there."

"You *what?*" roared Daviot. "Do you know the cost of that thing? You are a bloody moron. I am so deeply sorry, sir. I will take you back and we will settle this whole matter. Get the handcuffs off him, now!"

Hamish got a call from Jimmy Anderson, who gleefully related the whole scene. "It seems as if Harold reported you to headquarters for deliberately sabotaging his car and Blair came flying up. Harold insulted him. Blair arrested him and they're on their way back."

When she heard the story, Priscilla said in a voice as cold as the snowy scene outside the Land Rover, "I wouldn't put it past you, Hamish."

"Priscilla, I was nowhere around when the car wouldnae start. I thought someone was in trouble when a wee boy reported a woman was getting raped."

"So how did you get here so quickly from Braikie?"

"False report of a burglary."

Soon they heard the whir of a helicopter.

When it landed, Hamish got out and went to meet Daviot.

He noticed Charlie had disappeared.

"Report, Macbeth," commanded Daviot. Hamish said that a boy had reported a rape at the Falls of Shin and he had raced there. He found it was a false alarm. Then Harold's car wouldn't start so he had gone off to find a mechanic and had to wait until the man finished his dinner.

"I'll hae the keys," said the mechanic, and Harold passed them over. Soon they heard the engine of his car roar into life. "Seems just fine," he said. "Maybe your spark plugs got damp."

"Rubbish! The distributor caps had been stolen. Where is this schoolboy?" said Harold. "I don't believe he exists."

"Here," came Charlie's voice. He walked up to them leading two small boys whose faces were smeared with chocolate. "Go on, Declan," he said to one of the boys. "Tell the nice super-intendent what you saw."

"Me and Rory was up by the falls making a snowman," said Declan, "and we saw this wumman and a man seemed to be attacking her. I've got a mobile from my ma so I called the police."

Daviot turned to Priscilla. "Is there any truth in this? Were you in difficulties?"

Priscilla turned red with embarrassment. "My fiancé was kissing me, but I struggled free because it didn't seem the right place or time. I'm afraid these little boys got the wrong idea."

Harold rounded on Priscilla. "I am going back to civilisation right now. We are going to the hotel and then we are going straight back to London."

"Not here," said Priscilla. "We'll discuss this on the road back to the hotel."

"I want pay for my time," said the mechanic.

"You can take your time and stuff it up your highland arse," shouted Harold.

"Send your bill to police headquarters in Strathbane," said Daviot, "and maybe we'll call it quits."

"No, we won't call it quits," said Harold. "I'm suing you lot for wrongful arrest."

"It'll make a right amusing story for the

press," said Hamish, "when it gets to court. London stockbroker reported falsely for trying to rape his fiancée. Arrested and taken off in handcuffs. Although nothing up with his car, told hardworking mechanic to shove his bill up his arse. I can see the headlines now."

"Oh, drop the whole thing," said Harold.

He helped Priscilla into his car and drove off. Daviot nodded curtly to Hamish and climbed into the helicopter.

"Make that bill a big one," said Hamish to the mechanic. "Come on, Charlie. Do the kids live nearby?"

"Aye, they'll be all right. A croft just ower the brae."

"We may as well follow them. We're all going to Lochdubh anyway."

As they drove along, Hamish asked, "How much did it cost you?"

"Two bars o' chocolate and a fiver."

"Parents all right with that?"

"The father, John Sweeney, is a friend o' your mother's. No trouble at all."

"That's them up ahead," said Hamish, looking down the long road. "I don't like this. I think he's a brute. Priscilla's always looking for someone suitable to please her parents. Now what's happening? He's driven off the road and up thon forestry track. We'd better follow them."

"I wouldnae do that," said Charlie. "You'll give Harold a good reason to say we're stalking him."

"You're right," said Hamish. "You stay here and I'll go on foot."

"What on earth are we doing here?" demanded Priscilla.

"It's time you got to know who's boss in this relationship," said Harold. "Get in the back-seat."

"No, I will not. Drive me back to the hotel immediately."

Harold leaned across her, flicked open the glove compartment, and drew out a knife. He held it to her throat. "Do as you're told."

Priscilla wrenched off her engagement ring and threw it in his face. "The engagement is over." She opened the car door and got out. "I'll walk."

Harold got out as well, seized her, and threw her down in the snow. He brandished the knife. "You are going to do exactly as you're told, you frigid bitch."

The next moment he was seized by the collar and jerked backwards. Hamish Macbeth stamped on his wrist. Harold let go of the knife. Hamish picked it up and threw it off into the trees.

"I am charging you with attempted rape," said Hamish, "and with carrying a dangerous weapon. You—"

"Hamish," pleaded Priscilla, "let it go. I can't bear the scandal. I feel like an absolute fool. Please, Hamish."

"Oh, all right," said Hamish. Harold was still lying on the ground. He gave him a vicious kick in the ribs to relieve his feelings. "Go down to the road, Priscilla. You'll find Charlie there. I'll join you in a moment."

He walked to Harold's Range Rover and took the keys out of the ignition. "You can walk back to the hotel, you scunner," he raged.

He put the keys in his pocket and strode back down the track.

Harold had to wait two hours before the Automobile Association, already overloaded with emergency calls, managed to get someone out to him. He was freezing because without his car keys, he had been unable to put on the car heater. By the time he had thought to phone the hotel manager and ask that someone should go up to his room and find his spare keys, Hamish had already been on to the hotel. He was told that his cases were packed and waiting for him in the hall and he was no longer welcome.

Hamish kept Priscilla at the police station until he heard that Harold had left. He then asked Charlie to take her back. Priscilla was badly shaken. She had told him that Harold had seemed so romantic. He had sent her roses and taken her out to the best restaurants in town. Hamish felt he was listening to a description of a psychopathic control freak. He had heard of cases where men like Harold would start off as loving and caring. But usually they waited until the woman was secure in marriage before they started making life a hell.

Would Priscilla ever realise that there was something up with her? He remembered when they were engaged, how her coldness had made him want to weep.

He was just settling comfortably in front of the television with Lugs and Sonsie beside him on the sofa when his mobile rang.

It was Fiona. "I'll be with you in an hour. There's a lot to discuss."

Chapter Nine

"Come, come," said Tom's father, "at your time of life,
"There's no longer excuse for thus playing the rake—
"It is time, boy, you should think of taking a wife"—
"Why so it is, father—whose wife shall I take?"

—Thomas More

By the time the inspector arrived, Hamish was fast asleep. Fiona had let herself in. She stood looking down at him and made to shake him awake. The cat's eyes blazed with a yellow light and she let out a warning hiss.

"Macbeth!" Fiona shouted.

"What?" Hamish struggled awake and then got to his feet. "Sorry, ma'am. It's been a long day."

"Where's Carter?"

"At the hotel."

"Get him here!"

Charlie arrived in ten minutes' time, glad to escape from a dinner with the Halburton-Smythe family. Priscilla was miserable and her parents looked wretched.

He shied like a large carthorse when he saw Fiona, but all she said coldly was, "Now you are here, Carter, we can get down to business." She took her laptop out of its case and switched it on. "Here's what I have found. Yes, Andrew and Greta Harrison were at this wife-swopping party. The people who indulge in that sort of thing! There was even a judge there."

"Not your husband, I hope," said Hamish.

"Don't get cheeky with me, Sergeant. Now, how this sleazy party works is that they draw out slips of paper, and whoever's name's on it chooses a partner. It's a great big place out at Morningside. That couple go off to one of the many bedrooms. But the one who was not chosen was Greta because there was one woman too many. What did she do then? Nobody knows. Her husband tried to swear she was waiting for him when he had finished his business. That was how he put it. But all the others, now terrified of scandal, and promised secrecy provided they were honest, all swore that Andrew had left alone. She could have driven to the hunting box, lured Gloria outside, and strangled her. She and Andrew may have been terrified that old Harrison would leave everything in his will to her.

"I am keeping quiet about this for the moment until we talk to her. That will be all. I will see you both here at nine in the morning."

"How do you feel about her now?" Hamish asked Charlie.

"I don't feel anything. In fact, it's all like some sort of dream. Herself will be staying at the hotel. Maybe I should stay here."

"Oh, you'll be all right," said Hamish. "She's taken to calling you Carter and there was anything but lovelight in her eyes when she looked at you."

When Charlie returned to the hotel, he asked the night porter if he had a key for the door at the top of the basement stairs.

"I'll look in the office," he said. He was only away a few minutes before coming back and handing Charlie an old-fashioned rusty key. He had a job turning the key to lock the door but at last succeeded.

Half an hour later, the night porter looked up from the sports page of the newspaper he was reading to find Fiona Herring in front of him. She held out an imperious hand. "I need the key to the basement," she said. "The door is locked."

"Mr. Carter locked it," he said. "But there's nothing down there but old rubbish apart from Mr. Carter's wee flat. Can I get you anything?"

"No. I can wait until morning," said Fiona harshly.

Charlie awoke very early the next morning to get down to the police station before Fiona. The night porter was about to go off duty. "Oh, Mr. Carter," he said. "Thon inspector wanted the key to the basement last night, but I told her you had it."

Charlie blushed red. "Oh, it's nothing but

work with that woman," he said, and made his escape.

Hamish was up early as well and listened in dismay to Charlie's news. "The trouble is," said Charlie, "she might want to get her own back by saying I wasnae living in the station."

"I think she'd be too frightened to do that," said Hamish, putting a frying pan on the stove. "If she's got her wits about her, she might be worried you'd bring a case of sexual harassment. Sit down. What we both need is a good breakfast."

After a large fry-up of haggis, black pudding, eggs, and bacon, Charlie took a saucer and poured milk into it, and then salt into another.

"What the hell are you doing?" demanded Hamish.

"I'm putting this out for the fairies," said Charlie stubbornly. "I'm going to ask them for another blizzard. That way, we cannae go up there and I'll hae another day where I don't have to look at her."

"You're daft."

Charlie disappeared. When he came in, he

tripped over the dog, clutched the kitchen table, and fell down in a rain of crockery.

"Och, get a dustpan and brush," said Hamish, helping him to his feet. "You should have asked the wee folk to help you stop breaking up my home. Hurry up, man. It's nearly nine o'clock."

Charlie hurriedly cleaned up the mess and had just finished when Fiona walked in.

"Any sign of snow, ma'am?" asked Charlie.

"No. Make me a strong coffee, Macbeth, and then we'll get off. You can both follow my car."

They had just crossed the humpbacked bridge leading out of Lochdubh when a great gust of wind rocked the Land Rover and then the view ahead disappeared in a blinding snowstorm. Hamish gave a superstitious shiver and felt like crossing himself.

Fiona's driver turned her car into the hotel car park. Her driver got out and rapped on the window of the Land Rover. "The inspector says we can do nothing today," he said. "She will call you when the storm is over."

"A reprieve," said Charlie. "I'll keep to the station all day."

"I keep hoping Priscilla will be all right," said Hamish. "I sent Lochy a photo of Harold so he knows what he looks like. I also told him what happened."

While Harold was still stuck by his car, Priscilla had gone back to the hotel, packed her bags, taken a cab to Inverness airport, and caught a flight to London. She could not bring herself to face her parents with another broken engagement.

Upon her return, she switched on the television and settled down for a quiet evening. That whole episode with Harold seemed like a horrible dream. She switched on the news. She saw a report that an enormous blizzard had blanketed the north of Scotland and passengers had to be lifted off by helicopter from the Wick-to-Inverness train.

Harold stood outside on the pavement, swaying slightly, for he was very drunk. He wondered if Priscilla had changed the locks, for she had given him a set of keys. He thirsted for revenge. He walked into the entrance hall of the flats.

Priscilla had been so glad to be back in her flat that she had failed to either change the locks or to tell the porter to stop Harold from entering.

Harold nodded to the porter and made his way up the thickly carpeted stairs to Priscilla's flat on the first floor.

The porter stared as a huge man like a heavy-weight boxer strode into the hall.

"Here! Where are you going?" he demanded.

Lochy flashed a fake warrant card and growled, "Police." He strode up and listened at the door. Silence. He took out the keys he had been given and quietly opened the door.

He heard movement from a room at the end of the corridor. He gently tried the door. It was locked. Oh, well, thought Lochy with a mental shrug. Here goes. He raised one metal-capped boot and kicked the door open. Harold was in the act of handcuffing Priscilla to the bed.

Harold swung round. Lochy gave him a sav-age uppercut and knocked him unconscious.

Priscilla stared up at him, speechless with horror.

"There now," said Lochy soothingly. "Let's get you out of this. Charlie Carter told me to look after you, lassie." He unfastened the handcuff and helped her to sit up. "Do you want to call the police?"

"Yes. No," said Priscilla. "The newspapers. The scandal."

"All right, miss. I'll just handcuff this bastard. Right. Got anything to tie his feet?"

Priscilla climbed out of bed and staggered over to a drawer where she extracted a leather belt. "That's the ticket," said Lochy. "You'd better get the locks changed and a burglar alarm. Do you want me to get rid of this?"

"Don't kill him," said Priscilla through white lips.

"I'm no' in the killing game. But I wouldnae mind a wee dram."

"Of course," said Priscilla weakly. "Come through to the sitting room."

She led the way and Lochy lumbered after her. She poured a generous measure of

Glenlivet into a glass and handed it to him, then poured one for herself.

"I feel so stupid," she mourned. "I should have changed the locks. What happens now?"

"I'll take him away somewhere and make sure it disnae happen again."

There came thumps and yells from the bedroom. "Didnae hit him hard enough," said Lochy. "Back in a minute."

He went into the bedroom and took a roll of tape out of his pocket, sliced off a section, and pasted it across Harold's mouth.

Then he returned to the sitting room and picked up his glass. "That should shut him up for a minute. Aye, it was Charlie and Hamish were right worried about ye and asked me to keep an eye on ye."

"I must pay you something."

"No, your pa did that."

Priscilla began to cry. "I'm useless," she said at last.

"We all make mistakes," said Lochy sententiously. "Now, I'd better do my job and get him out of here."

"Won't the porter call the police?"

Lochy grinned. "He thinks I am the police."

He went back to the bedroom and ripped the tape from Harold's mouth. "I've got a gun," said Lochy. "One peep out o' you and you're a dead man." He unfastened the belt from round Harold's ankles but kept the handcuffs on him.

Harold in all his bullying life had never known such terror. He allowed Lochy to march him past the porter without saying a word. Outside, Lochy shoved him into the passenger seat of his car, got in himself, and drove off.

"Do you want money?" pleaded Harold.

"I want you to shut up. There's brandy in the glove box if you need some Dutch courage."

"I'm handcuffed."

"Poor wee soul." Lochy jerked the car to a halt. He fished out the flask of brandy, opened it, and held it to Harold's lips. Harold took a great gulp, not knowing it was heavily drugged. In no time at all, he was fast asleep.

Lochy drove steadily northwards until he reached one of the less salubrious parts of Birmingham. He stopped his car, went round, and hauled Harold's body out of the car, took off the handcuffs and dumped him on the pavement, and then drove off.

Harold awoke at dawn the next morning. He stumbled to his feet and looked wildly up and down the deserted street. He tried to find out the time but discovered his gold Rolex had gone. Terrified, he felt in his pockets. No wallet, no phone, no driving licence. Nothing.

He saw a sanitation truck coming down the street and stood in the road waving his hands for it to stop. He shouted that he had been mugged.

"You'll find a police station round the next corner," said the driver.

Harold thirsted for revenge. But outside the police station, he stopped in dismay. If he told them about Lochy, the man would be arrested, but the whole story of his own attempted rape would come out.

He squared his shoulders and walked in. He told the desk sergeant that he had been drinking in a pub in London when someone must have slipped him a mickey. The next thing he knew, he had woken up in a Birmingham street to find he had been mugged. It seemed to take ages to give a statement to a detective. Then a wait until the firm he worked for started for the day to confirm his identity and say they would send a car for him.

At last, having been told to take the day off, he returned to London to find his apartment had been burgled. He sat down amid the chaos and began to phone to cancel all his credit cards and phone the insurance company and the police.

Charlie was awakened during the night by a call from Lochy and listened in horror to his story of the attempted rape. Before Fiona arrived at the station, he told Hamish what Lochy had said.

"What's up with her?" howled Hamish. "Why does she always pick losers?"

Charlie politely forbore from pointing out that Hamish himself had been one of the losers.

Fiona arrived. "The snow has stopped and I

think we can make it," she said briskly. "I don't like all this havey-cavey stuff but we'll need something concrete to take to Daviot."

"All she had to do is deny it, ma'am," said Hamish.

"We'll interview her on her own and see if we can break her."

"Fairies aren't working today," said Hamish as they followed Fiona's car. The snow ploughs and gritters had done a good job. It was still dark because in winter in Sutherland the sun only crept over the horizon around ten in the morning.

"Don't mock the wee people," said Charlie.

They made their way slowly to the hunting lodge. A grey dawn was beginning to cover the sky as they moved up the now familiar drive. Juris answered the door and told them that the family were at breakfast.

"We wish to interview Mrs. Harrison," said Fiona. "We will use the study."

They seated themselves in the study and waited. Greta walked in, followed by her husband.

"We wish to speak to your wife alone," said Fiona.

"This is an outrage," spluttered Andrew. "I shall phone Mr. Daviot and—"

"Do that," said Fiona, "and I will make sure the newspapers find out how you and your wife pass your time in Edinburgh."

Andrew beat a hasty retreat. Hamish surveyed Greta. She was a big powerful woman with strong hands.

"Mrs. Harrison," began Fiona. "You were odd woman out at that wife-swopping party. You could have left and driven up here to strangle Gloria Dainty."

"Why on earth would I want to do that?"

"Perhaps you were afraid your father-in-law might change his will and leave everything to Miss Dainty."

"I never even met the woman," snapped Greta.

"When you left this Edinburgh party, where did you go?"

"I went back to the George Hotel and went to bed. I ordered room service. The staff will be able to vouch for me."

"Why did you leave?"

Greta suddenly looked weary. "I don't like the games Andrew likes to play. I find it all rather sad. But do check up on me by all means and if that's all you've got, get the hell out of here."

They looked at each other after she had left. "I've an awful feeling her alibi will check out," said Fiona.

"What about the statements from the druggies?" suggested Hamish. "We could pull them in."

"As you pointed out earlier, Mr. Daviot is so determined the case is closed," said Fiona, "that he will simply insist that drug addicts will say anything. It's a dead end. I've got time owing. I am going to Edinburgh for a break. A word in private with you, Carter. Wait outside, Macbeth."

Hamish waited in the hall. Fiona came out after a few moments. Her colour was high. She did not speak to Hamish but went on through the hall, out into the snow, and slammed the door behind her.

"What happened?" asked Hamish when Charlie came out of the study.

DEATH OF A NURSE 261

"Just a private matter," said Charlie. "Let's go."

Christmas came and went. The New Year dawned. Hamish and Charlie went about their duties. Only Charlie was happy. He and the colonel spent a great deal of time together. Hamish, however, felt the murders were unsolved. The fact that there might be a murderer out there, feeling safe and secure, kept coming back to haunt him. After Christmas, Andrew and his wife had gone back to London.

Then one fine day, he saw Juris and his wife coming out of Patel's shop. "How is Mr. Harrison?" asked Hamish.

"Same as ever," said Juris. "His son and daughter-in-law are coming up next weekend on a flying visit."

"Is Mr. Harrison leaving you anything in his will?" asked Hamish.

"Oh, he says he is. But he tells everyone around he's leaving them money. It's to keep us all sweet. But the lawyer was round last week. I listened at the door. Andrew gets it all. I told

the gamekeeper, Harry Mackay, and the shepherd, Tom Stirling. You should ha' seen their
faces. The old man had promised them the
ownership of their cottages and a good sum
when he died, because it's no secret Andrew
plans to sell the place off. Man. Harry was that
furious, he said he felt like putting a bullet in
the old man."

"And what about you?" asked Hamish.

"Oh, me and Inga never believed him. I mean,
it's right typical of rich old people. They promise this one and that one to keep them all
running around."

Hamish uneasily watched them both go. He
hoped Mr. Harrison's promises would not turn
out to be a sort of Russian roulette and someone might be tempted to help him to an early
grave.

Chapter Ten

Life is one long process of getting tired.
                              —Samuel Butler

As a few weeks of rare fine weather continued, Hamish was almost able to put the murders out of his mind. He had dutifully called on Miss Whittaker and the accountant, Gerald Wither, to give an account of the closing of the case—an account he could not quite believe in.

He had a niggling worry to plague him which had nothing to do with the murders. He was walking his pets accompanied by Charlie when a pretty hitchhiker approached him and cried, "A wild cat! I never thought to be so close to one."

"It iss not the wild cat," said Hamish, his accent becoming stronger as it did when he was distressed or worried. "It is chust the large tabby."

The girl was small, carrying a huge pack on her back. She had curly fair hair dyed with streaks of shocking pink and a cheeky face.

"Suit yourself," she said. "But that's a wild cat and it should be with its own kind. Unnatural to keep it as a pet."

She waved to him and walked on, leaving Hamish worried. He looked down at Sonsie. Would the cat really be better in the wild? And what would become of Lugs without his friend?

"What do you think?" he asked Charlie.

"Maybe she's right," said Charlie awkwardly. "I'm always afraid that one day someone's going to take you to court and get the beast. We could take her ower to Ardnamurchan and let her loose. If she doesnae run away, well, that's that. We'll take her home. But maybe give her a chance o' freedom."

"Oh, leave her be," said Hamish.

But the next day, something happened to

change his mind. He had forgotten about Blair's long campaign against him. The detective chief inspector's wife, Mary, had been reading about the extension of the Ardnamurchan sanctuary. She showed Blair the article, saying, "Doesn't that wild cat look like Hamish's pet?"

Blair studied the article and his bloodshot eyes gleamed with malice. When his wife had left to meet friends, he found the e-mail address of the trust and informed them that one local policeman in Lochdubh was keeping a wild cat as a pet.

Fortunately for Hamish, a scientist and his assistant called at the hotel first for lunch and told the waiter that they were going to the local police station because there had been a report of a wild cat. The waiter told the manager, who phoned Hamish. Charlie took Sonsie off. Hamish ran to the vet and borrowed a large domestic tabby and sat down to wait.

The scientist and his assistant when they called were plainly disappointed. When they left, Hamish had a sudden intuition that Blair was behind it. He managed to get Mary on the phone when Blair was out and asked her if her husband had shown any interest in wild cats.

"Funny you should say that," said Mary. "I was looking in the papers about the wild cat sanctuary and there was a photo and I said to him that it looked like your cat. He grabbed the paper and shot out the door."

When he had rung off, Hamish put his head in his hands. He knew Blair would never give up. Somehow, the wretched man would get a photo of Sonsie and then the game would be up. When Charlie returned, he told him what had happened.

"Well, now," said Charlie. "We'll drive to Ardnamurchan and let her out. If we're stopped, we can say we're going to visit the lighthouse. If she comes back, we'll take her home and find some way to get Blair to shut up."

Ardnamurchan is wild and very beautiful with only a sparse population. The tip of the peninsula—Britain's westernmost point—extends between the islands of Mull to its south and

Eigg, Rum, and the more distant Skye to its north.

They had left Lugs at the hotel in the care of the chef. A magnificent sunset was blazing across the sky as they followed a one-track road, looking nervously to right and left in case any scientists leapt out of the heather.

"Here'll do," said Hamish, pulling onto the side of the road. "We'll settle down and light the stove as if we're having a picnic and see how Sonsie reacts."

"Cats are very territorial," said Charlie. "What if she gets mauled?"

"Then her attacker is going to be one stun-gunned cat."

Hamish got out and lifted out the stove. "I brought sausages," said Charlie, producing a pack. "Sonsie is right fond of sausages."

"Grand," said Hamish, feeling suddenly cheerful. He felt sure Sonsie would not leave him.

Soon the sausages were frying and Charlie was pouring cups of coffee from a thermos. "Let the cat out, Hamish," said Charlie. "We'll need to try sometime."

Suddenly uneasy, Hamish let the cat out. Sonsie's great head turned this way and that and then she bounded off across the heather.

"She'll be back," said Hamish. "I'll put a couple of sausages on a dish for her."

They waited and waited. Then Hamish whistled, that whistle that had always brought Sonsie running back, but there was nothing but the sound of the breeze soughing through the weather.

The stars blazed overhead. "I'd better go and look for her," said Hamish.

Charlie put a hand on his arm. "Something's there. Sit right quiet."

Creeping out of the heather came Sonsie and what looked like a great wild tom cat. They grabbed a sausage each and fled back into the heather.

"I think that's that," said Charlie. But Hamish would not be moved. Charlie got a sleeping bag out and made himself a bed in the heather, but Hamish sat all night long, his heart heavy.

When Charlie awoke in the morning, he

found Hamish slumped against the side of the Land Rover, fast asleep. He gently shook him awake. "Come on home. It's all over."

"What about Lugs?" asked Hamish on the road back.

"We'll see if the vet has any strays," said Charlie. "Get him a wee puppy to look after. You get some more sleep and I'll see to it."

Hamish awoke later in the day. He and Lugs walked slowly along the waterfront. Charlie's car screeched to a halt. He got out carrying a small white poodle in his arms.

"Meet Fifi," he said proudly.

"That's no dog for a man," said Hamish. "Take it away."

"Oh, Hamish. It belonged to old Mrs. Murchison what died last week and no one wants her wee pet. It's got no home."

Charlie put the poodle down. She pranced up to Lugs and nuzzled his ear.

Lugs licked her face.

"See?" said Charlie. "Isn't she cute?"

"I'm not having any animal called Fifi."

"Then call her something else."

"Look, Charlie. Okay. So long as Lugs is happy. Could you settle them in and feed them? I've got to be somewhere."

All day long, Hamish sat in Ardnamurchan where he had left Sonsie and called and whistled. Night fell and still he waited until he fell asleep.

In the morning, stiff, cold, and miserable, he drove the long way back. As he drove along the waterfront, he saw Charlie standing in the middle of the road, waving his arms.

"Just in time," said Charlie. "Got a call. Andrew Harrison has been murdered!"

It became clear to Hamish and Charlie when they arrived at the hunting box that they were no longer to be privileged investigators. Fiona, Jimmy, Blair, and two detectives were waiting outside for the forensic team to finish their work and for the pathologist to give his report.

Fiona swung round when she saw them and said loudly and clearly for all to hear, "Your presence will not be necessary. Get back to your normal duties."

Blair gave a fat grin. "Well, that's that," said Hamish as they both climbed back into the Land Rover. "Talk about hell having no fury."

As they drove off, Daviot was arriving.

In the rearview mirror, Hamish saw Blair taking Daviot to one side.

Despite all the detective chief inspector's frequent gaffes, Daviot felt comfortable with him. They were members of the same lodge. Blair always kowtowed to him and never made him feel like a fool.

"It looks as if Malky could not have been the murderer," said Daviot.

"Isn't that just what I was thinking," said Blair eagerly. "And I know who's to blame for that."

"Who?"

"Our inspector. Didnae you think it weird, sir, that instead of investigating the murders with professional detectives, she should go out on her own and demand the presence of two local highland bobbies?"

"Yes, that does seem strange," said Daviot. He had not liked Fiona's high-handed attitude.

"I mean, sir, the police commissioner would be quite shocked if he heard. There were rumours around that she was sweet on Carter and her a married woman and to a judge, too."

"Keep your eye on things here," ordered Daviot. "I'm going back to police headquarters."

Once back at his desk, Daviot sent a long e-mail to the police commissioner, putting the blame for pinning the murders on Malky fair and square on Fiona's shoulders. He felt a warm glow of gratitude towards Blair, feeling that the detective had managed to exonerate him, Daviot, from blame.

In the police station, Hamish absentmindedly patted the little poodle and scratched Lugs's ears. His dog looked up at him out of his odd blue eyes. "Sorry, old boy," said Hamish, "but Sonsie isn't coming back."

"I'll make us some tea," said Charlie.

"Good idea." Hamish stretched and yawned. "Then I think I'll catch up on more sleep. I'm so tired I can't think straight. Do me a favour, Charlie, and take Lugs and that other ridiculous animal out for a walk after we've had some tea."

"You'll have to give the wee poodle a name."

"I'll call it It for the moment."

"What about Frenchie? Pretty wee thing."

"If you want."

They drank their tea in silence. Then Hamish said slowly, "Fiona is going to be in trouble over this."

"Why?"

"Just a feeling. As we drove off, I saw Blair talking to Daviot. Daviot won't want to take the blame for a botched case. What if it came out that she took us around with her, instead of proper detectives?"

"She seems to have a lot of power. Probably won't come to anything. I'm off. I'll wake you later. It's a good thing old Harrison didn't promise to leave us something in his will or we'd be dragged in for questioning as well."

"They won't get far," said Hamish. "Juris won't tell Blair a thing once he starts his usual shouting and bullying."

*   *   *

Charlie walked the animals, glad in a way to be off the case and away from Fiona. The little poodle was a big hit with the locals. Even the Currie sisters bent down to pet her. He then drove them up to the hotel, had a cosy chat with the colonel, and promised to go fishing with him the next day.

When he returned to the station, he saw with a sinking heart that Fiona was sitting in her car outside. She got out and waited while he parked and let the dogs out.

"I've been suspended," she said abruptly.

"Why, ma'am?"

"Some malicious bastard put in a report that instead of using highly trained detectives, I was covering the case with two highland coppers. I mistakenly relied on reports of Macbeth's successes."

"Ma'am, he was the one who told you that I did not think the murderer was Malky."

She looked at him sullenly, got into her car, and her driver drove off.

"Will Daviot call us in for an explanation?"

asked Charlie when he had told Hamish what had happened.

"He can't," said Hamish. "He knows damn well we were following orders and that he went along with it. I'm sick o' the whole business. I need to think. I'll do some chores."

"I'll help you," said Charlie.

Hamish was well aware that Charlie was capable of breaking more things around the station. "No, you take the day off," he said. "I'll phone you if I think of anything."

Hamish went indoors, made himself a cup of coffee, and then went into the office to go through his notes on the computer. Lugs came in and put a paw on his knee and stared up at him. "She isnae coming back," said Hamish sadly. "You'll just need to make do wi' that piece of fluff called a poodle."

After a few minutes, Hamish heard the large flap on the kitchen door bang. He rose and went through to the kitchen to get a piece of shortbread. He looked out of the kitchen window. Lugs and the poodle were chasing each other round the back field in the sunshine.

I wish I could get ower the loss of Sonsie that easy, thought Hamish.

He went back to the office, put his hands behind his head, and stared into space, letting all the scenes from the investigation run through his head. Forget about old Harrison's will, he thought. I wonder if his life was insured. I wonder if they needed money. But Andrew must have been making a fair whack as a London barrister. But maybe Greta was sickened by the sex games. Still, if she wanted rid of her husband, surely the time to do it would have been at the height of the murder investigations.

How had Andrew been murdered and where? He phoned Jimmy on his mobile.

"I'll lose my job if they know I'm talking to you," whispered Jimmy.

"How was Andrew murdered and where?" asked Hamish.

"Savage blow to the head out in the grounds. Look, get the whisky ready and I'll drop in on you later."

After he had rung off, Hamish began to think about drugs. Malky had been a good-looking young man to judge from the photos of him published in the newspapers. He had been handsome enough to attract Gloria and help her get the job with Harrison. Why hadn't that nursing agency noticed if any of their drugs were missing? They must keep some on the premises. It didn't seem likely. And surely nurses couldn't write out prescriptions.

He had a sudden urge to see if there was a chemist near the nursing agency. He phoned Angela and begged her to look after the dogs.

"I heard Sonsie has gone and you've got a poodle," said Angela. "I'll look in at the station. What's the poodle called?"

"You think o' something," said Hamish. "Thanks, Angela."

Hamish called first at the hotel and asked Charlie if he could borrow his car, not wanting to alert Strathbane that he was on their patch.

He parked near the clinic and looked around. There was a small chemist's a few yards away. Hamish went in and asked the girl behind the counter if he could speak to the pharmacist.

The pharmacist introduced himself as George Stoddart. He was a tall, thin man with a face as white as his coat and a shock of white hair. He looked as if he had been bleached all over.

Hamish asked if he could remember a nurse called Gloria Dainty coming in with prescriptions. "The one that was murdered? Yes, I remember her. She used to collect medicine for patients."

"Is it possible you could find out from your records what the prescriptions were for and which doctor signed them?"

"Wait a minute. It shouldn't take long."

He went into the back where a computer lay on a desk in front of shelves of medicines. Hamish waited impatiently. It was a quiet residential area. Customers came and went. Hamish noticed the computer had a huge back on it instead of a flat screen. Probably take an age even to warm up, he thought.

At last the pharmacist came back. "The prescriptions are all from Dr. Strachan."

"Where is his surgery?"

"Blythe Road, just round the corner."

"And what were the prescriptions for?"

"Methadone and diazepam. It seemed odd to me that she would want such a quantity, but Dr. Strachan said it was all in order."

Hamish walked out into the sunshine and made his way round the corner to the surgery. The waiting room was full, but he flashed his warrant card and demanded to see the doctor immediately.

He was ushered in after a patient had left. Dr. Strachan rose to his feet and held out his hand. "Welcome. How can I help the police?"

He was a small brown-haired man, somewhere, Hamish judged, in his forties. He had a square, pugnacious face.

"The nurse Gloria Dainty received a great number of prescriptions from you for methadone and diazepam," said Hamish.

The doctor studied his hands, which were large with thick fingers. "As part of her job. She needed the stuff for patients."

Hamish loomed over him. "Rubbish," he

said. "Before she went to Mr. Harrison, she had one patient and that was Miss Whittaker. Tell me what is going on or I will report you to the medical council."

He buried his head in his hands and then looked up. "We had a brief fling," he said. "She wasn't a patient of mine and she came on to me strong. Then it was over, but the pharmacist phoned me to query prescriptions brought in by her. I called her and demanded an explanation. She said she had stolen a prescription pad from me but if I said anything, she would go to my wife and she had the photos to prove it. She had taken some photos on her phone when we were...er...fooling around. I couldn't bear the scandal. Officer, if this gets out, I'll lose my job, my wife, and my children."

"I think I can keep quiet about it," said Hamish. "But if it becomes relevant to an investigation I'm on, then I'll need to say something."

"Oh, God bless you," said the doctor, and he began to cry.

*   *   *

So, thought Hamish, as he drove back north. That doesn't really get me any further. I knew already that Gloria was supplying Malky with drugs. If I report it, I'll get a row for not telling police headquarters that I was going to Strathbane. They'll arrest the doctor and maybe decide it was he who murdered Gloria. That's just the sort of thing Blair would do.

It all goes back to Harrison and his damn will. That's the only reason for bumping off Andrew.

As he climbed down from the Land Rover outside the station, Angela came to meet him. "That poodle is so sweet," she said.

"Not a man's dog," said Hamish huffily.

"Neither is Lugs," pointed out Angela. "I mean, Lugs is not a working dog, like a sheepdog. Have you ever thought that attitude is why you have so much trouble with women?"

"What are you talking about?"

"Gloria Dainty was a shallow gold digger. But you never saw that; neither did any of the other men in the village. All you saw was the blonde hair and the sexy outfit. Until you learn to look below the surface, you'll never get married. There's some ordinary-looking woman out there with a good heart and you wouldn't even give her a second look. That's why you keep missing out."

Hamish stared at her. Angela, with her gentle face and wispy hair, did not turn heads and yet Hamish had always thought the doctor fortunate in his choice of wife. But there was something in what she said. Something he had missed.

"I wonder," he said. "I just wonder."

He turned abruptly on his heel and marched into the police station. The poodle jumped up and down in welcome and Lugs rattled his food bowl. Still turning over what Angela had said, Hamish fried up venison liver for the dogs. He waited until the meat had cooled, chopped it up, and put it down in their dishes.

The kitchen door crashed open. Jimmy walked in, pulled out a kitchen chair, and sat down. "I deserve a dram, Hamish. What a carry-on! Herring goes off, threatening us all with the wrath of God, Blair shouts and bullies,

Greta in tears, lawyer called, Blair charged with police harassment, and everyone screaming and cursing and yelling."

Hamish poured him a dram of whisky. "And what did Helen Mackenzie have to say for herself?"

"What? The boot-faced nurse? Why? She's the only one in the clear."

"Harrison has gone round promising everyone money in his will, even the shepherd. What about Helen? How did he get her?"

"You remember, when Gloria was murdered, he said he phoned for a replacement and they sent Helen."

"I remember. I'd like to know more about Helen. She must have known Gloria. Jimmy, I've been warned off. Why not ask the agency if there was any friendship between Gloria and Helen?"

"Not me. After today, I'm not taking the initiative in anything."

After Jimmy had left, Hamish drove up to the hotel and went down to Charlie's apartment. He and the colonel were sitting by the fire.

"I thought Charlie had time off," complained the colonel.

Hamish ignored him. He told Charlie about his concern about Helen Mackenzie, Harrison's nurse whom they had never once suspected. Had the colonel not been such a fan of Poirot, he would have gone off in a huff. But instead he listened intently.

"The trouble is, we're stuck," said Hamish. "We daren't show our faces in Strathbane now."

To his surprise, the colonel said, "My wife is going to spend a week with friends in Helmsdale. What if I employed a nurse from the agency? Then I might be able to get all the gossip."

"But you're as fit as a fiddle," said Charlie.

"I can pretend to have had a fall."

"That would be grand if you could do that," said Hamish.

"Anything for Charlie," said the colonel, eyeing him coldly.

The colonel went upstairs to phone. The agency said it would normally be difficult to find a nurse for only a week, but fortunately Nurse Betty Freeme was just between jobs and could attend immediately. She would bring the necessary papers with her.

The colonel sat back at his desk, feeling excited. He could see all the suspects gathered in the library and he would say, "You did it!"

Chapter Eleven

Many a woman has a past, but I am told she has at least a dozen, and that they all fit.

—Oscar Wilde

Betty Freeme was a sturdy woman in her late twenties with ginger hair, freckles, and pale-blue eyes. She did wonder why the colonel needed a nurse. He asked to be pushed around in a wheelchair, but any suggestion of bathing him or putting him to bed was met with horror. At last, she decided he was lonely with his wife being away. He seemed to want to talk a lot.

The colonel got her to talk about the agency

and then asked if the late Gloria Dainty and Helen Mackenzie had been friends.

"Oh, them!" laughed Betty. "I'd say they hated each other. They were all right for a bit. Both were working locally and got together on their nights off. Then Gloria started dating that chap Malky, the one who murdered her, and I saw them out in front of the agency one day shouting at each other, but I couldn't hear what they said."

"And what did the police say when you told them this?"

"They didn't ask me. It's just gossip anyway. I mean, Helen is one of the strict-type nurses, everything by the book. I couldn't ever understand her friendship with the likes of Gloria. Gloria was flighty. Goodness, it's not yet dark, sir. I'll just pull those curtains back."

"Leave them!" shouted the colonel. "The light hurts my eyes. Ask one of the waiters to bring me a whisky and soda."

Betty reached for the phone. "No," barked the colonel. "You'll lose the use of your legs. Get it from the bar."

When she had gone, Charlie and Hamish emerged from behind the curtains. "Ask her if Helen has any family," said Hamish. "We need to find a lot more about her."

Charlie and Hamish retired behind the curtains as Betty returned with the drink.

"The reason for all these questions," said the colonel, "is because I am a friend of Mr. Harrison and he is in a terrible state over the killing of his son. I trust this Helen will look after him?"

"She's highly qualified, I believe," said Betty.

"Got family in Scotland?"

"I remember she said she was an orphan, but she sometimes took time off to visit her aunt in Kinlochbervie."

"What is the aunt's name?"

"I forget. But the aunt was her father's sister and hadn't married, so she'd be a Miss Mackenzie."

"I might take a run up there tomorrow," said the colonel. "I really am concerned for Mr. Harrison's welfare."

"You could ask the agency for her details," said Betty.

"No, no. I couldn't do that. Run along now. I'll ring if I need you."

When she had gone and Hamish and Charlie had emerged from their hiding place, the colonel said excitedly, "Kinlochbervie! Now there's a coincidence. I'll go up there and—"

"No!" exclaimed Hamish. "If by any chance Helen should turn out to be a killer, you'll be next. Leave it to me and Charlie."

"Please, George," begged Charlie. "It could be awfy dangerous. Hamish and I will go up there."

After they had left, the colonel sat in his wheelchair, feeling frustrated. He had this rosy dream of unmasking the killer.

He had to move quickly before his wife came back to demand what he was doing in a wheelchair. Then he hit on it. There was nothing to stop him paying a visit to old Harrison. He would get Betty to drive him over. Harrison would surely be sympathetic to what he would see as a fellow sufferer. And he could have a chance to examine Helen closely. He rang the bell.

✳   ✳   ✳

On the road to Kinlochbervie, Hamish and
Charlie discussed how they should approach
the aunt. "We don't want to alert Helen," said
Hamish.

"We could say there's been a report of a couple of burglaries," said Charlie, "and we're just
going from door to door."

"Aye, that might just do," said Hamish. "I
hope your friend George leaves things alone."

"Nothing he can do," said Charlie. "We're on
the only lead."

By asking around, they finally located Miss
Mackenzie's home. It was a small bungalow, a
box of a place, on the outskirts of the village.
There were no flowers in the garden fronting
the house, only two squares of grass intersected
with a brick path.

Hamish tucked his cap under his arms and
rang the bell. A tall, gaunt woman answered
the door, leaning on two sticks. Hamish introduced them and explained about the fictitious
burglaries.

"The first I've heard of it," she said. "But

come ben. I've just put the kettle on and I never have much company."

She led the way into a sunny front room. A comfortable old sofa and chairs flanked a low coffee table. In one corner was an old-fashioned television set and in another a set of shelves crammed with paperbacks.

"I'll get the tea," she said. "Sit down."

"I'll help," said Charlie.

"I can manage."

When she had left the room, Hamish looked around. There were no photographs. Above the fireplace was a Russell Flint print. The carpet was beige and fitted. An arrangement of pinecones decorated the fireplace. Outside, the wind had risen and they could hear the noise of waves on the beach and the scream of the plunging and flying gulls. A newspaper pressed against the window as if staring in before being whipped away again by the wind.

Miss Mackenzie came back in pushing a laden trolley, her two sticks lying on the bottom ledge. Charlie would have risen to help, but Hamish put a hand on his arm to stop him. He was frightened that clumsy Charlie might start breaking things.

She handed them each a thin china cup decorated with roses. They waited patiently until she poured cups of tea and handed round a plate of scones before recovering her sticks and lowering herself into an armchair.

"Arthritis?" asked Hamish sympathetically.

"Bad today," she said. "My niece is a nurse and she was supposed to bring me some medicine."

"Who would that be?" asked Hamish.

"Helen. She's working for a man called Harrison down near Braikie."

"That's where all those murders have been," said Hamish. "Aren't you worried about her?"

"No, she's as tough as old boots. Turned out well, mind. I used to worry about her."

"And why was that?" asked Charlie.

"Oh, she was a bit o' a handful at one time. My poor brother and his wife were killed when their house went on fire and Helen was put out to foster parents. I wasn't considered suitable, being a maiden lady. Mind you, I had her here on holidays until... Well, never mind."

"Lovely scones," said Charlie. "Light as a feather. Did she do something bad?"

"It was odd. I had this cat, Tufty. I was right fond of it. Helen was only eight. I used to smoke. I had one of those Ronson lighters you fill with petrol. Helen was out in the garden one day. I looked out of the window. She poured petrol over the cat and set it alight. I couldn't believe my eyes. I sent her packing and told her never to call again. But she turned up last year and told me she was a qualified nurse, and she cried over Tufty and said she must have been jealous of my affection for the cat. After that, she called from time to time and brought me drugs for my arthritis."

"Was an awful business about that poor second sight woman being killed," said Charlie.

"Oh, poor Jessie McGowan. Never harmed a soul. Now, what about these burglaries?"

Hamish gave her a fictitious story. "It's drugs," said Miss Mackenzie when he had finished. "The pushers are always looking for new markets."

"Did you ever consult Miss McGowan yourself?" asked Hamish.

"No, the poor woman was mad. Helen believed in that rubbish."

They thanked her and went outside and drove out of town to the café on the beach where Hamish let the dogs out to play. He watched them sadly. He could not banish the hope that one day, he would look up and see Sonsie playing with them.

They ordered coffee and sat looking at the glassy waves curling on the beach. "What about this," said Hamish. "Maybe Malky was romancing the two of them to get drugs. But he drops Helen for Gloria because he's thought up this scheme with Gloria of trying to get old Harrison to leave her money in his will, or even to marry her. Helen set that cat on fire. Psychos often start off with killing animals. She gets Gloria out of the way. Then she hears about the witness in Kinlochbervie and gives her a present of wine laced with antifreeze.

"Now, we know Harrison is an old scunner. He treats everyone like dirt. But he's led Helen

to believe that she'll get something in his will.
Then she finds out it all goes to Andrew. So
out goes Andrew. Harrison will be a shattered
man and might begin to cling to her. But surely
she must come under suspicion. Now that your
friend George has done his bit, I hope he keeps
out of it."

"Oh, he'll be all right. What can we do
now?" asked Charlie.

"We wait until the dust settles and keep an
eye on the lodge until, say, next Sunday when
Helen gets her day off, and see where she goes
and try to have a word with her."

"Got a name for the poodle yet?"

"Cannae think o' anything," said Hamish.

"What about Bella? Pretty wee thing."

"I'll think about it."

Betty Freeme heaved a sigh of relief as she
turned into the drive leading to the hunting
lodge. The colonel had criticised her driving
every few yards. She pulled up in front of the
house, glad the journey was over.

Juris answered the door and to the colonel's

request said that Mr. Harrison was not seeing anyone. The colonel handed over his card. "He'll see me," he said. "Hop to it."

They waited in the hall. Betty wished they could leave. The hall was as dark as usual with only glimmers of light shining on the glass eyes of the stuffed animals. The wind moaned around the building like a banshee.

Juris came back. "He can give you a few moments," he said.

Betty seized the handles of the wheelchair and pushed the colonel towards the drawing room.

Mr. Harrison was seated by the French windows, staring out. Helen was standing on guard behind him.

"Colonel Halburton-Smythe," announced Juris.

Harrison slowly turned round. "What's up with you?"

"Strained my back," said the colonel. "I'm sorry for your loss."

"Well, well," said Mr. Harrison, his old eyes bleak. "He wasn't much of a son but he was all

I had and now he's gone. I wish I'd never come to this cursed place. As soon as the coppers are finished, I'm selling up and going back to Yorkshire. I should never have left."

"Will you be taking your staff back with you?" asked the colonel.

"Probably not. I'll always wonder if it was one of them who killed my poor son. Helen, make yourself useful and get me a whisky and soda."

The colonel studied Helen, but her face was like mask.

"Is there anything I can do to help?" asked the colonel. "Perhaps you might like to stay at the hotel as my guest? Change of scene and all that."

"I'll think about it," said Mr. Harrison fretfully. Helen handed him a whisky and soda and he took a great gulp. "That's better. I'll never know what came over Andrew."

"What did he do?"

"He was trying to get power of attorney. Said I was past it. I told him I'd see him in hell first. Mind you, I blame Greta. Always plotting and scheming to get my money."

Juris came in. "The police are back again, sir."

"Oh, God, will this never end? Sorry, Colonel, but I might take you up on that offer."

"Anytime," said the colonel. "You are lucky to have such an efficient nurse."

"Oh, Helen's all right. Only one around here I trust."

To Betty's surprise, when they arrived back at the hotel, the colonel told her he did not need her services any longer. He assured her she would be paid for the whole week.

When Charlie and Hamish joined him later, the colonel was bursting with ideas. Hamish was, however, alarmed. "You're putting yourself in danger," he said. "If Harrison accepts your invitation, then Helen will come to the hotel with him. Then there is Harrison himself. He can walk. Andrew trying to get power of attorney might have turned his brain and the wretched Helen might be his accomplice. Let's hope he doesn't turn up."

The following Sunday was one of those grey days in the Highlands when all colour seemed to have been bleached out of the landscape. All was silent except for the occasional mournful call of a curlew. Hamish and Charlie in plainclothes, and with Charlie at the wheel of his old car, lay off the road near the hunting box and waited. At last, they saw a small Ford with Helen at the wheel driving past. She did not notice them. They gave her plenty of time to get ahead and then set off in pursuit. She drove steadily on and took the road to Strathbane. Fortunately, there were one or two cars on the road and Charlie hung well back.

"I wonder if she's going to the agency," said Hamish.

"Why?"

"She might want to get in touch with Betty and find out all about the colonel."

"Let's hope not," said Charlie.

They followed Helen to the agency, parking carefully round the corner. "We'll watch until she leaves," said Hamish, "and then go in and see if we can find out what she was trying to find out."

He peered round the corner, but after only a few moments, he said, "She's out again. There's a truck coming along. Tuck in behind it, Charlie, so she doesn't see us."

After a few streets, the truck turned off, leaving them feeling exposed. Charlie hung back before setting off again in pursuit. Finally Helen stopped outside a large villa on the outskirts. Again, Charlie parked around a corner. Hamish got out to discreetly watch the villa. Helen was inside for a quarter of an hour before coming out again and getting in her car.

"Right," said Hamish. "Let's go in and see if Betty is working there."

It was Betty herself who answered the door. She looked at them in surprise as Hamish produced his warrant card and said they would like to speak to her.

"Only a few minutes," said Betty. "I've just started work here and my gentleman will be wanting tea soon."

She led them into a gloomy Victorian front parlour dominated by a large stuffed owl in a glass case. The room was cold and damp.

"We wondered why Helen Mackenzie called on you," said Hamish.

"I'd been working for Colonel Halburton-Smythe," said Betty. "Helen said she was tired of Mr. Harrison and wondered if the colonel would be needing a new nurse. I told her there seemed to be nothing up with him and he was all right now. She asked if the colonel had been curious about the murders and I told her everyone was. That's all. I've really got to go."

Hamish begged her to say nothing about their enquiries, and he and Charlie took their leave.

"I don't like this at all," said Hamish. "We've got to keep an eye on the colonel."

They went back to Lochdubh and straight to the hotel to find the colonel triumphant with news. Mr. Harrison had phoned him and had decided to accept the colonel's invitation to stay at the hotel.

"That nurse Helen had been asking questions about you," said Hamish. "She may not hesitate to murder again."

"Pooh! Charlie will look after me," said the colonel.

But Hamish fretted. "There's so many ways

she could get at you. Poison, a blow on the head, anything."

Mr. Harrison was allocated one of the large rooms on the ground floor. Its barred windows looked out over the back. Hamish saw that there were several laurel bushes outside the windows and decided to watch and see what happened when Helen was alone with her patient. If only, he thought, they had enough on her to get a search warrant. And yet her room at the hunting lodge had been searched twice along with all the other rooms.

He and Charlie were told they could have dinner that evening, but at another table. To Hamish's dismay, he heard the colonel moving into Poirot mode and beginning to question Harrison and Helen all about the murders. They were on first-name terms, but at last Harrison seemed to weary of all the questions and said sharply, "Look, George. I am still mourning the death of my son. I don't want to talk about it." The colonel reluctantly dropped the subject. Helen did not contribute to the conversation.

When Harrison retired for the night, Hamish went out to take up his post outside the bedroom window. It had begun to rain, steady drenching rain, pattering down on the laurel leaves and dripping down the back of his neck. To his dismay, thick curtains had been drawn across the windows. He pressed his ear to the glass.

"I think you would be more comfortable in your own home," he heard Helen say.

"Nonsense," came Harrison's voice. "The food's great here and I need a change of scene. Leave me. I'm tired of your fussing around."

"Now, then. What would you do without your Helen?"

"Find another nurse. Like taxis in a rank."

"Now, aren't we cruel? You said you loved your Helen."

"Oh, shove off. I want to be on my own. I wish George would stop playing detective. I believe he thinks you're a murderer, Helen. What do you think of that?"

"I could sue him."

"You wouldn't get very far. He suspects everyone."

✳   ✳   ✳

The days dragged by. Harrison finally took his leave. Nothing sinister had happened. A FOR SALE board was now outside the hunting lodge. The days were sunny, just the sort of weather that Hamish usually enjoyed. But the dark shadow of unsolved murders plagued him. He was sure Helen Mackenzie was a ruthless murderer.

Charlie and the colonel were sitting one evening in Charlie's apartment when the colonel said, "I feel Percy Harrison should really be warned about that nurse."

"We've no real proof," said Charlie. "Helen's got an aunt in Kinlochbervie. The second sight woman was killed there. She and Gloria were both dating Malky, we think, and no doubt supplying him with drugs, but we've no proof. We've proof Gloria was doing it but nothing on Helen. We think Helen bumped off Gloria so she could get her job and maybe woo Harrison herself, but she looks like the back of a bus. So surely no hope there."

"I think I should give him a clear warning," said the colonel.

Hamish came clattering in wearing his big boots. The colonel looked at him crossly. He didn't like Hamish interrupting his cosy evenings with Charlie.

"George is thinking of giving Harrison a clear warning about Helen," said Charlie.

"Is Greta still in residence?" asked Hamish.

"I believe she went south after the funeral," said the colonel. "You surely don't suspect her?"

"I think it's all about money," said Hamish. "If Harrison dies, then surely Greta inherits."

"Maybe not." The colonel brightened. "I could just ask him who he's leaving his money to now."

"Oh, keep out of it," said Hamish wearily.

"I am not taking orders from some useless copper who had the damn cheek to jilt my daughter," raged the colonel. He got to his feet and stomped off up the stairs.

The colonel set out for the hunting lodge the next day. He asked Harrison to dismiss Helen, saying he wanted to talk to him in private about a serious matter.

The day was sunny and warm and the long windows were open onto the terrace.

"It's like this, Percy," began the colonel, and he plunged into a long story about why he suspected Helen of being a murderer. He ended up by saying, "If I were you, I'd put it about you haven't signed a will. That should keep you safe."

"I'm leaving Helen money in my will," said Harrison. "And I'm taking her to Yorkshire with me."

"Why? You could get any amount of nurses."

Harrison grinned. "I'm telling you, Percy, Helen does the best hand job in the Highlands."

"Is that a type of massage?" asked the colonel.

Harrison rocked with laughter and then told him in graphic detail exactly what a hand job was. The colonel turned bright scarlet. "I've got to go," he said hurriedly. He fled from the hunting lodge, followed by the cackle of Harrison's laughter.

The colonel did a detour to the florist's in Braikie and bought his wife a dozen red roses, thanking God for his clean life and a decent wife.

Charlie called in at the police station that evening to tell Hamish about the colonel's adventure. When he had finished, Hamish sighed. "I'm sick o' the whole business. Let her bump him off in Yorkshire and let the police down there sort it out."

"Not like you, Hamish. When did you last have a holiday?"

"Can't quite remember. I don't usually bother when things are quiet like this. Slope around. Take things easy. Heard anything of Fiona?"

"Not a word."

"Jimmy's not come near me, either. I mean, surely they must know now it couldn't have been Malky. But the way I see it, they got such a bruising in the press that the last thing they want is to open up that can o' worms again."

"We could be looking in the wrong place," said Charlie. "Could ha' been Juris or Greta."

"No, it all points to Helen. Damn! I cannae leave it alone. Do you know what I'm going to

do? I'm going up there and I'm going to tell
Helen I think she committed the murders."

"She'll report you to Strathbane. She'll sue
you. You'll lose your job."

"So what? I cannae go on in the job wi' this
hanging over me. Something's got to break."

"I'll come with you."

"No. One of us in trouble is enough. Take
the dogs with you for the day."

Hamish set out for the hunting lodge. He could
feel his fury against Helen mounting. He found
Harrison and Helen in the drawing room and
told Harrison sharply that he had called on police business and wanted to see Helen Mackenzie
alone. Mr. Harrison protested, but Helen said
she was sure it would only take a few moments.
Harrison shrugged and wheeled himself out of
the room.

Helen sat primly on the edge of an armchair
and Hamish pulled up a hard chair and sat opposite her.

Helen's eyes were flat and cold and betrayed
neither interest nor curiosity.

Hamish began. "I know you murdered Gloria Dainty, Jessie McGowan, and Andrew Harrison. Maybe you killed Willie Dunne as well. You killed Gloria to get her job so that you could seduce Harrison into either marrying you or leaving you money in his will. When you learned he had left it all to Andrew, then Andrew had to go. If that old fool Harrison does make out a will leaving money to you, he will be next. Here's what I have found out so far."

As he talked, she sat there, unmoving, her reddened hands folded on her uniform lap.

When he had finished, she stood up and said coldly, "I am going to report you to your superiors."

"Please do," said Hamish, "and tell them exactly what I have said."

"And I am going to sue you."

"Grand. The newspapers will have a field day. Hear this: I'll be watching you every step o' the way."

Hamish turned and left the room. As he got to the front door of the hall, he had a feeling of being watched. He swung round but could see no one in the shadows.

He suddenly felt lighter and freer. He had burnt his boats. Now let's see what she will do.

Two days later, Hamish received a call from Juris. "The nurse has disappeared," he said. "All her stuff is in her room, but she's gone."

"I'll get over there," said Hamish. He called Charlie. Then he phoned Jimmy and explained what had happened.

"I can't say anything about confronting her," said Hamish as they sped off. "I'll be hauled over the coals. Damn! Did she run for it? But why leave her belongings behind?"

As if to suit his mood, black rain clouds were being driven in from the west on a rising gale. The gamekeeper was on guard at the gates to keep the press at bay. How did they find out so soon? wondered Hamish. A small huddle of men stood in the now driving rain.

Juris let them in. "We'll interview you after we've seen her room," said Hamish. "We cannae go in because we'll need to leave it clear for forensics, but we can stand at the door and look in."

They followed Juris up the shadowy stone staircase. Outside the wind had risen to an eldritch scream. Lightning flickered across the glass eyes of the stuffed animals, and then came a great roll of thunder. Juris went on up to the second floor and pushed open a stout oak door.

Hamish peered in. He put a handkerchief over his hand and switched on the light. Not much had been changed since the days when it had probably housed a governess. There was a single brass bed against the wall with a side table, holding a Bible. By the opposite wall was a toilet table with an old-fashioned ewer and basin. No wash hand basin with running water. Beside it stood a large Victorian wardrobe, the door standing open to reveal coats, dresses, and skirts. There were no books or pictures. The mullioned windows let in very little light.

"Right, Juris," said Hamish. "We'll go down to the study and start the questioning."

But as they descended the staircase, there came a pounding at the door. Juris hurried to open it. Blair, Jimmy, several policemen, and a forensic team crowded in.

"We'll take over," said Blair. "There's enough o' us here. You pair, get back to your station."

Hamish and Charlie climbed into the Land Rover. Hamish stared moodily out at the pouring rain. "This is all wrong," he said. "Why should she leave her belongings behind? I didn't see a handbag in that room. Maybe she took her money and cards and left. Let's go to the garage. I want to see if her car is there."

He reached into the back for his oilskins and shrugged into them before getting out into the storm. Followed by Charlie, he made his way to the garages, which had been converted from the old stables.

Hamish swung open the door and went into the musty interior, smelling of petrol, oil, and dust. "That's her car," said Hamish. He took out a pair of latex gloves and slipped them on. The car was not locked. He flipped open the glove compartment. Nothing but a roll of peppermints. He opened the boot. It was clean and empty. He studied the tyres. There was no sign that the car had been driven recently. In fact, the car looked as if it had been recently washed, inside and out.

"Now, did she get it washed herself or did someone else? Where's the nearest car wash, Charlie?"

"Nothing till you get to Strathbane," said Charlie. "Fine Foods supermarket on the outskirts."

"Let's try there," said Hamish.

The whole of the Highlands seemed to be in motion as they drove south to Strathbane. Lightning stabbed down and thunder rolled. At one point, their way was blocked by a fallen tree and they had to bump over the moor to get round the blockage.

As they neared Strathbane, the sky began to clear to the west, and by the time they drove into the supermarket car park a watery sun was shining down.

The manager said they did not take a note of car registrations at the car wash, only entered the type of cleaning required in the books. The cars were all washed by hand by a gang of Eastern Europeans. Hamish asked to see the security tapes for the past two days.

He and Charlie settled down in the manager's office to go through them. But after hours of searching, there was no sign of Helen's car.

Charlie scratched his head. "You seem to be thinking something nasty happened to her," he said. "But she's the main suspect."

"It's the way she left," fretted Hamish. "Leaving it all behind, even her car. And why was that car so clean inside and out? Is there any other car wash?"

"Not that I know of," said Charlie. "There'll be one in Inverness."

"Too far. It would show some signs of mud by the time it was brought back."

"Couldn't she just have asked Juris to clean it for her?"

Hamish phoned the hunting box. When Juris answered, he asked him if he had cleaned the nurse's car and was told firmly that he had not. "It is not my job to work for the help," said Juris with all the haughtiness of a stage butler.

"Let's get something to eat," said Hamish. "I'm starving and I cannae think on an empty stomach."

They found a café which sold all-day breakfasts and tucked into fried haggis, black pudding, eggs, bacon, tomatoes, and mushrooms.

"Think the dogs will be all right?" asked Charlie.

"They'll be fine," said Hamish. "I left them dog food but Lugs has probably introduced the poodle to the delights of the Italian restaurant's kitchen. Now let's think. Just suppose Helen has been murdered. Let's try that one. Who would murder her and where would they dump the body?"

"Well," said Charlie slowly, "the only one who might have it in for Helen is Greta. What if she found out that Harrison had changed his will in Helen's favour?"

Hamish phoned Juris again. When he had rung off, he said, "Greta is in residence. Harrison has refused another nurse and says Greta will look after him. She's been there for the last week and she's a powerful woman. Maybe she guessed Helen had bumped off her husband and took her revenge. I hate being out o' the loop. It's like detecting in Victorian times, Charlie. They could have found all sort of hairs and DNA and we don't know about it."

"If you wait until this evening when all the reports are in," said Charlie, "I could try my hand at hacking into Blair's report and the forensic reports."

"So for now let's try to figure out where Helen's body could have been dumped," said Hamish. "That car bothers me. So clean. Let's try this way. Someone kills Helen and uses her car to dump the body. It's a wee Ford, not a four-by-four, so no use for going over the moors. So the body would need to be dumped near a road. And whoever would not want to be away from the hunting lodge for too long."

"That drug business bothers me," said Charlie. "I mean, say she was in some drug racket, then someone from Strathbane could have got rid of her."

"Maybe, but would they use her car and then

get it cleaned? Let's get back up there and start searching."

They drove back to outside the hunting lodge. "Right or left, I wonder," said Hamish.

"Let's try left," said Charlie. "The instinct would be to veer left away from the road to Braikie."

The days had drawn out and they knew the evenings would be light and that they had plenty of time for their search.

But they could find no trace of anything. "Let's call on Dick," said Hamish. "He might have some ideas."

Dick gave them a warm welcome, but to Hamish's disappointment, the beautiful Anka said she had orders on the computer to work on and left them to it.

Over excellent mugs of coffee and scones, Hamish told Dick all he knew.

"There's a car wash here now," said Dick. "At that wee garage. Couple o' Poles. You could try there. Do me a favour. At the bottom of the stairs, there's a big bag o' cans. Could you dump them at the recycling unit? You know where it is, Hamish. Out on the Lochdubh road before you get to the new seawall."

They thanked him for the coffee and made their way to the garage. But it was shut up for the night and no one around could tell them where the Poles lived.

"I'm weary," said Hamish. "Let's get rid o' Dick's rubbish and start again tomorrow."

The recycling unit was considered a disgrace because it was rarely cleared. Great mounds of cans, bottles, and newspapers reared up against the evening sky.

Seagulls swooped and dived. Two seagulls fought over a hamburger wrapper. Silly birds, thought Hamish. No food there. He dumped the sack of cans on top of a pile of others.

A seagull shat on his regulation sweater and he shook his fist at it. He made to turn away. Something was bothering him although it was hard to think with all the noise of the waves crashing on the shore and the wheeling, screaming birds. He turned slowly round, looking to right and left. A supermarket trolley had been dumped at the far end of the unit. It was over-flowing with cans and plastic bottles. Nothing sinister there apart from one black shoe.

Hamish unhitched his torch from his belt and walked forward. One black regulation shoe. He began to claw at the cans and bottles, send-ing them flying.

Stuffed in the very bottom of the trolley was the dead body of Helen Mackenzie.

Her empty eye sockets stared up at him.

The seagulls had had her eyes.

Chapter Twelve

How often have I said to you that when
you have eliminated the impossible,
whatever remains, however improbable,
must be the truth.
                    —Sir Arthur Conan Doyle

Blair was furious. Had Daviot not been on the scene, he would have suspended Hamish from duty for destroying valuable evidence by throwing the cans and bottles which had covered the body all over the place.

"Why is it," Daviot asked Jimmy, "that one highland policeman can find out what we have missed?"

"Maybe it's old-fashioned policing," said

Jimmy. "Hamish doesn't have any of the bene-
fits of forensic science and so he has to use his
brain."

A crowd had gathered outside the recycling
unit, their faces avid with curiosity in the lights
of the halogen lamps which had been erected.

Helen's body and the supermarket trolley
were now shielded inside a tent. "She's been
strangled," whispered Hamish to Charlie.
"Bruises on her neck and her poor face black. I
wish these seagulls would go away. I hate them."

"I think they'll be here when we're all gone,"
said Charlie. "I mean, that's the creepy thing
about Sutherland when you're out on your own
under the stars. You feel like an intruder. But
the birds belong."

Jimmy came up and demanded a full report.
He listened carefully to Hamish's story about
the car. "Get back into Braikie," he ordered,
"and see if you can find where that garage
owner lives and then find those Poles."

They found the garage owner lived in the bottom half of a house near the garage. He was

sleepy and cross at being woken up, but he volunteered that the Poles lived in a bed-and-breakfast at the back of the garage.

The door of the B&B was opened by a small woman wrapped in a tatty dressing gown and with her hair in rollers. The minute she saw their uniforms, she began to shriek that she kept a respectable house. Charlie told her in a soothing voice that they simply wanted to speak to her Polish residents.

"First floor left," she said sulkily. They made their way past her and up the stairs. The car washers turned out to be two brothers. They were not Polish but Lithuanian and their English was not very good. But with patient questioning and showing them a photo of Helen's car, which Hamish had snapped on his phone, they volunteered that a man had driven it in two days ago. They described him as being tall and dark and dressed in jeans and a T-shirt. He had been wearing a baseball cap pulled down over his eyes.

"That doesn't sound like anyone we've come across so far," said Charlie gloomily as they left.

"We'll need to come back in the morning,"
said Hamish, "and ask all around."

He reported back to Jimmy, who told him
to write up what he'd got and see if he could
find out anything else. Blair was holding an im-
promptu press conference, swollen up with ego
like a bullfrog until a reporter asked him what
Strathbane thought about the mistake in pinning the murders on Malky, upon which Blair
abruptly stalked to his car and got driven off.

In the morning, Charlie arrived with the news
that Mr. Harrison had phoned and wanted to
book himself and his daughter-in-law into the
hotel. He said he was weary of what seemed like
a constant police presence.

"George has said he'll try to get as much information out of him as possible," said Charlie.

"Let's hope the colonel is careful. If our murderer comes for Harrison, he might take out
the colonel as well. You'd better nursemaid
them, Charlie, and I'll cover for you. I'll get
back up to Braikie and see if I can find out
more about our mysterious car cleaner."

Before he left, Hamish took the dogs for a walk. He met the Currie sisters and, remembering how rude he had been to them, blurted out an apology.

"What you need is a good woman," said Nessie.

"Good woman," echoed Jessie.

Hamish touched his cap and hurried on. Nessie scampered after him. "There's the widow Banks up at the churchyard at the grave of her wee boy what died of meningitis. She would make a man a good wife. Rosie Banks needs to move on."

Hamish looked across at the churchyard where a woman was slumped in front of a gravestone.

"I'll maybe have a word with her later," he said, and made his escape.

He had taken photographs of everyone at the hunting box on his iPad. He set out for Braikie. The landscape was glittering from the recent rain. He glanced up at the mountains, steel grey against the washed-out sky, noticing every gully and crag sharply defined, and knew that was a sign of more rain to come.

He had not taken his pets with him. Since the loss of Sonsie, he did not feel the need for their constant company. He often thought about Sonsie and mourned the loss of his big cat.

He went straight to the car wash and showed the photographs to the two Lithuanians. They studied. them closely and then one of them pointed to the photo of Juris. "Maybe," he said.

"Was he Eastern European like you?" asked Hamish. They said he hadn't spoken, merely handed over a piece of paper asking that the car be cleaned inside and out.

"Anything odd about the inside?" asked Hamish. "Bloodstains? Signs of violence?"

They looked at him, puzzled.

Hamish went to the translation app on his iPad, typed in a series of questions, got them translated into Lithuanian, and passed them over. They typed back that the boot had been muddy. Nothing in the car but a scarf.

What had they done with the scarf? Handed it over when the man came back for the car. What did the scarf look like?

Paisley pattern.

Hamish wondered how he could get Juris on his own. Police would still be combing the hunting box for clues. Then he remembered that Juris always answered the phone.

He rang him up and said he wanted to talk to him away from the house and suggested Juris drive to a pub called the Drop Inn in Braikie.

The pub was thin of customers. A brewery had tried to encourage more customers by turning it into a gastropub, but it seems the hard drinkers of Braikie preferred the dinginess of the Red Lion. He took a table by the window and waited. He was just beginning to think Juris would not come when he saw him parking outside.

Juris joined him and asked abruptly, "What's up?"

"You know Helen's body has been found?"

Juris nodded. "Do you mind if I have a beer?" he asked.

Hamish went to the bar and got him a pint. He stared straight at Juris and said, "Why did you have Helen's car cleaned?"

He expected a hot denial but Juris said calmly, "It's my job."

"What!"

"Look, Mr. Harrison has a mania about clean cars. That includes Helen's. I protested before that I wasn't there to be a servant to a nurse and he told me to obey orders. It was my job. So I check the garages as usual and there's her wee car covered from top to toe in mud. So I took it to the car wash. Got a receipt and put it down on my expenses."

"When did you find the car?"

"It was the morning before we found she'd disappeared."

"And did you report this to the police?"

"It's like this. That man, Blair, is out to pin it on me because I'm a foreigner in his eyes. If I told him, he would have dragged me off. You know he would. That's why I lied to you and told you I hadn't had the car cleaned."

"You could be accused of tampering with evidence," said Hamish.

"I was only doing my job as usual," said Juris stubbornly.

"Describe the car."

"Like I said, it was top-to-bottom in mud. Helen was a bit of a slob and the inside was full of sweetie wrappers and old beer cans. I looked in the boot and it was all muddy."

"There was a scarf. Do you have it?"

"It's in my car."

"I'll need that. I'm sorry, Juris, but you're in for a rough time. I'm afraid I'll need to call Strathbane. That could have been the scarf that strangled her. I'll try to get Jimmy Anderson to deal with it."

After Hamish had called Jimmy, he was told not to let Juris out of his sight. He, Jimmy, would take Juris in for questioning.

Jimmy eventually arrived with two police cars following.

Is he really innocent? wondered Hamish. Or am I leaning backwards against Blair's hatred of foreigners?

There seemed to be nothing else to do but go back to Lochdubh, look over his notes, and hope there might be just something he had missed.

As he drove along the waterfront, a thin drizzle was beginning to fall. He saw that Mrs. Banks was still in the graveyard. He stopped his vehicle and got out.

He walked up to her and said gently, "You'll get soaked. Come away, lassie. There's nothing you can do now but move on."

She was a plump little woman in her thirties with rosy cheeks, cheeks that were now blotched with tears. She had lost her husband to cancer and then immediately afterwards, her six-year-old to meningitis.

Hamish helped her up. "You need bereavement counselling," he said. "Go and see Dr. Brodie and he'll fix you up. Would your husband and boy want you to live like this?"

She scrubbed her eyes with the back of her hand and sighed. "I almost envy folk whose bairns are murdered."

"Why?"

"Because when the murderer is caught and punished, that's closure."

"I think that's a television fiction," said Hamish sadly. "If it's a child, there is no closure. Just courage. I'll walk you to the doctor's now."

After he had delivered her to Dr. Brodie, he walked through the rain and up to a hill overlooking Lochdubh to where his first dog, Towser, was buried. He sat down on the wet heather and stared at the simple cross that marked the dog's grave. How he had grieved over the loss of Towser! How he had sworn never to have another pet. But Archie had given him Lugs and then the vet had given him Sonsie.

Hamish sat there for a long time until he realised he was soaking wet.

He made his way back to the station and changed into civilian clothes. A seed of an idea was beginning to take place in his brain. It was farfetched. It was outrageous. But somehow, it fit.

He phoned Charlie and said, "Call down here. I've an idea and I need your help."

The colonel was sitting with his wife, Mr. Harrison, and Greta when Hamish arrived with Charlie.

"We would like a word in private with Mr. Harrison," said Hamish. "May we use the manager's office?"

"You can't walk in here and order me around," said the colonel.

"Please, George," said Charlie quietly. "It's important."

"Oh, very well. Push me along, Greta."

"It's all right. I can manage," said Hamish, seizing the wheelchair.

The office was lit with a shaded green lamp on the desk. Hamish took out a powerful tape recorder and laid it down on the desk.

"What's up with you?" snarled Harrison.

"Mr. Percy Harrison," said Hamish. "I am charging you with the wilful murder of Helen Mackenzie."

"Why on earth would I kill the bitch?"

"Grief," said Hamish. "She killed your son. You overheard me accusing her of the murder of Andrew and of Gloria and Miss McGowan. Andrew was your only son. Somehow, you shook a confession out of her and then you strangled her. You can walk. I know that. I saw you once. You're a powerful man. You waited until the middle of the night, maybe slung the dead body over your knees in the wheelchair, and took the body out to her car and dumped it in the boot. You had strangled her with her scarf. You took the body to the dump, shoved it in an old trolley, and piled the trolley up with cans and bottles. You put the car back, knowing Juris would find it and clean it. You hated her so much, you didn't even bother to hide anything. You could have cleared out her room and made it look as if she had fled.

"But you had murdered her and got your revenge and that was all you wanted."

"You gormless idiot," roared Harrison. "What proof do you have?"

"Your DNA is on the scarf that strangled her," lied Hamish. He knew it would take ages for any results to come in. "Forensics took the DNA of everyone at the hunting box ages ago."

Harrison sat for a long time, staring at the lamp on the desk as if hypnotised. Then he said, "Yes, I did hear you. Andrew might be pompous but he was my son. I told Helen to wheel me over to the garage because I wanted to look for something. Then I got her by the throat. I said if she confessed, I would let her escape. If she said nothing, I would kill her. I took a gun and jammed it in her mouth until she nodded. She went on about how she thought I loved her. Rubbish. She said Gloria had always been scoring off her in the past and had taken her boyfriend away. One day, Gloria had called on her and shown her that diamond pendant I gave her. Helen wailed it just wasn't fair. She started pleading and babbling that she had done it all for me. That she had killed Gloria to protect me. I could have shot her then and there. But I put the gun in my pocket. I told her I would let her go if she came back into the house and typed out a confession.

"It seemed to take hours with her breaking off to try to justify herself and begging and weeping. She was the one who sent that filthy anonymous letter so that my last memory of poor Gloria was shouting at her. At last she was finished and I got her to sign it. She even confessed to wearing the scarf with which she had strangled Gloria. I made her fetch it.

"I stood behind her with the scarf around her neck and strangled her. It seemed right that she should die by the very scarf with which she killed my Gloria. I got into my wheelchair, slung her dead body over my knees, and went out to the garage. Why didn't I take one of my own cars? I didn't want to muck them with her filthy body. I crammed her in the boot. I had to break her legs with a tyre iron so that she would fit.

"I was going to dump her on the moors but her wee car couldn't cope with going off-road, and then I remembered the recycling place and thought it fitting she should end up with all the other rubbish."

He fell silent.

"I will type out a statement for you to sign," said Hamish. "You will now be locked in your room until reinforcements arrive from Strathbane. Charlie, go ahead and search for that gun."

"He won't find it," said Harrison. "I left it in the safe in the hunting box."

To Hamish's relief, they made their way to Harrison's room without encountering anyone. Harrison gave Hamish the statement from Helen. Hamish locked him in, pocketed the key, then went back to the office and called Jimmy.

The colonel wondered what was going on. He went to the office and peered through the glass panels. He could see Hamish and Charlie sitting there. He asked the night porter where Mr. Harrison was, and was told he was in his room.

He knocked at the door and called, "Percy! Have you gone to bed?"

There was a silence and then Harrison's voice came from just behind the door. "The door's locked," he said, "and I could murder a whisky and soda."

"I'll have it open in a minute," called the colonel. "We use that room for friends. I keep a key under this big vase outside the door. People are always losing that key."

He opened the door. "I'll get you a drink from the bar. Won't take a moment."

The colonel felt that Hamish Macbeth was cutting him out from the investigation. He hurried to the bar and shouted for a whisky and soda.

When he got back to Harrison's room, the door stood open but there was no sign of the old man. The colonel hurried to the office. "Do you know where Percy is?" he demanded.

"He is locked in his room, waiting to be taken off to Strathbane," said Hamish.

"What! Why?"

"He has confessed to the murder of Helen Mackenzie and given me a statement from Helen Mackenzie where she states she was responsible for the other murders."

"But I unlocked the door for him," wailed the colonel.

Hamish and Charlie rushed out of the office. To their demands, the night porter said that Mr. Harrison in his wheelchair had gone out of the hotel.

Percy Harrison bowled along the road towards Lochdubh in his wheelchair. It was a balmy night with a small moon riding high overhead. He reached the humpbacked bridge and stopped.

The river was in full spate because of all the melting snow coming down from the mountains. The water roared and sparkled in the moonlight. He heaved himself out of his wheelchair, wincing as the pain from his back shot down through his legs. Gasping, he clung to the parapet. Far behind him, he heard the wail of sirens.

He leaned over the parapet and gazed hypnotically down at the racing foaming water.

As Hamish and Charlie rushed down to the bridge, Harrison gave his crippled body one monumental heave and plunged down into the river.

He suddenly decided he did not want to die. There was no death penalty. He struggled and fought as the strong current sent him tumbling down into the loch and pulled his body under.

Hamish ran down to the shore and stripped down to his underwear, wading into the loch. He began to swim towards where he had seen

Harrison disappear. He dived and dived again, searching in the blackness until his fingers grabbed hold of cloth. He hauled the body of Harrison to the surface and dragged it ashore and set about trying to pump the water out of the man's lungs.

But there was no sign of life. Harrison's eyes revealed no life at all, only the reflection of the stars above, causing a sort of false intelligence.

Hamish Macbeth was in disgrace. He began to feel like the murderer himself as the accusations from Daviot and Jimmy went on and on. Hamish could only be thankful that no one had been able to find Blair.

First Hamish was questioned at the hotel and then taken off to Strathbane with Charlie, where they were interrogated separately. Why was it, demanded Daviot, that two police officers locked up a confessed murderer and did not put a guard at the door?

On and on it went, all night long, until Jimmy took pity on Hamish. "Look, sir," he said to Daviot, "the media are going to give you a lot of kudos for solving the case. There isn't going to be a court case so it's best to leave Macbeth out of it. Just say the case is solved and that you have a taped and written confession and don't say how you came by them."

Daviot brightened. "Do you agree to that, Macbeth?"

"Yes, sir."

"Well, well, now. I may have been a bit hard on you." He turned to a police officer posted by the door. "I think we could do with some coffee here and some Tunnock's tea cakes."

When the coffee and cakes arrived, Daviot continued. "So. Why on earth did you think of Harrison?"

"Grief for a dead son," said Hamish. "I was sure Helen was the murderer and if Harrison thought she had murdered his son, he might take revenge." Hamish decided not to tell the superintendent about being overheard accusing Helen of the murders.

"I am sure we would have forensic evidence eventually," said Daviot, who had such faith in DNA and forensics that he had quite forgotten that police were supposed to use their brains and intuition.

Hamish and Charlie eventually returned to Lochdubh, agreeing to meet at the station at four in the afternoon when Daviot was to hold a press conference. Charlie went to the hotel and to his apartment, where he found an angry colonel waiting for him. The colonel's dreams of being Poirot had been shattered and he blamed Hamish for keeping him out of the investigation.

"I don't blame you, Charlie," said the colonel. "You have to follow orders. But that lazy long drip of nothing deliberately kept all the investigation to himself."

Charlie opened his mouth to say that Hamish was a police officer and the colonel had no standing whatsoever, but diplomatically remained silent to let, as he thought, the wee man get it out of his system.

Hamish was chased along the waterfront by the press, who had gathered at the bridge when he drove up. He dived into the station and ignored the batterings on the door.

He awoke later and shaved and dressed again. The press had given up, no doubt having gone to Strathbane for the press conference. Charlie arrived and they went into the living room and settled down to watch the conference on television.

Daviot, tailored and barbered, was flanked on one side by Jimmy and on the other by a grinning, smirking Blair.

He made a statement saying that Mr. Harrison before his suicide had confessed to the murder of Helen Mackenzie. Mr. Harrison had found out that Helen Mackenzie had murdered his son and so he had taken his revenge after forcing her to write a signed statement.

Then came the questions. How had the police suddenly come to the conclusion that Mr. Harrison might have murdered his nurse?

Daviot smoothed back his silvery hair. "We use our intuition," he said. "It is known as good old-fashioned policing."

Blair pushed forward to the microphone. "I

would like to say that all the credit for solving this difficult case is due to the efforts of Super-intendent Daviot."

"*Northern Times,*" called a reporter. "Was Hamish Macbeth anything to do with it?"

"Hamish Macbeth," said Daviot smoothly, "is merely one of our officers on the case. He is to be commended for trying to save Mr. Harri-son. That is all. No more questions."

"And that's that," said Hamish. "Well, at least there won't be any suggestions of promotion and moving me to Strathbane. Oh, damn, there's the door. Leave it. Probably some re-porter."

"Open this door immediately, Macbeth," called a peremptory female voice.

"Oh, God. It's Fiona," said Charlie.

Hamish went and opened the kitchen door. Fiona strode in.

"What the hell has been going on?" she raged. "Did you precious pair not think to keep me in the loop?"

"It's like this," said Hamish quietly. "There was no time to contact you in Inverness. It all happened so quickly. Sit down. Have a dram and I'll tell you all about it."

Hamish poured three shots of whisky and then began to talk. Fiona listened carefully until he had finished.

She said, "So because of your mistake in not guarding Harrison's hotel room door, you get no credit at all. That must rankle."

"It doesn't," said Hamish. "If I keep a low profile, then it means I can keep my police station here."

"I fail to understand an unambitious man," said Fiona. "Surely you, Charlie, don't want to be buried up here forever?"

"Suits me fine, ma'am," said Charlie.

"The pair of you are a waste of intelligence," said Fiona. "I'm off. Coming, Charlie?"

"I've got stuff to type up," said Charlie, his normally pleasant face closed down like a shutter.

Fiona stalked to the door and nearly tripped over the little poodle. "What a ridiculous dog," she said.

"Got a name for it yet?" asked Charlie when the door had slammed behind Fiona.

"Sally."

"That's not French."

"It's a British poodle," said Hamish. He bent down and stroked the dog's springy fur and thought of Sonsie with a sudden wrenching pang. He almost wished the wild cat had died to spare him the agony of constantly wondering how she was.

An hour later, the kitchen door opened and Jimmy walked in. "I saw Old Iron Knickers driving away," he said. "Bet she was in a right taking."

"Something like that," said Hamish. "So is everything quiet at Strathbane?"

"Aye. Daviot has almost come to believe he's a genius. I see the whisky on the table. Don't worry. I'll help myself. The things that go on up here in peasantville! Murderous nurses. Old boys in wheelchairs who can walk. What next?"

"Absolutely nothing, I hope," said Hamish.

Epilogue

I must down to the sea again, to the vagrant gypsy life,
To the gull's way and the whale's way
where the wind's like a whetted knife.

—John Masefield

The wrapping up of the murders seemed to take an immense amount of paperwork. At some point, Hamish Macbeth began to feel he would never, ever be able to return to his lazy life.

But at last it was all over and he and Charlie spent long lazy sunny days on their vast beat or out in the loch, fishing.

Down in Strathbane, Chief Detective

Superintendent Blair dreamt of winkling Hamish out of his station. Then one day he thought he had found a glimmer of hope. Blair was sure there had been something going on between Fiona Herring and Carter. If only he could get proof, then Carter would be removed and it would be one crack at least in that lazy Macbeth's life. Opportunity finally came his way one night when he was driving home. The car in front of him, a Jaguar, was slewing across the road. He drove in front of it, forcing the driver to stop.

From his gold Rolex to his Savile Row suit, the driver was just the sort of "posh git" who got up Blair's nose. He demanded his driving licence. The driver's name was Peter Tuck of London. He said he was booked into the Tommel Castle Hotel for a fishing holiday.

Blair breathalysed him and found he was well over the limit.

"Get out of your car. I am impounding it," ordered Blair. "You will come with me to headquarters, where you will be formally charged."

Peter was a florid middle-aged man, his face

covered in a sheen of sweat. He took out his wallet. "Maybe we can settle it here," he said.

"Are you trying to bribe a police officer?" roared Blair.

"Wouldn't dream of it, Ossifer," slurred Peter, putting his wallet away.

Blair liked bullying. And bullying posh people was something he really enjoyed.

Peter was locked up in the cells for the night to sober up and was told he would be up before the sheriff in the morning.

During the night, Blair began to wonder if he could put this drunk to use. The man would be staying at the hotel. As a guest, he could talk to the staff and find out if there had been anything going on between Fiona and Charlie Carter.

A sober and frightened Peter listened to Blair's suggestion. "If you do this for me," said Blair, "you can have your car and licence and we'll say no more about it." Peter readily agreed.

Blair stared at him out of his piggy bloodshot eyes. "Talk to anyone about this arrangement," he said, "and I'll have ye. Get it?"

"Yes, yes," said Peter. "Just get me out of here."

By the time Peter had checked into the hotel and was settled in the bar with a large whisky, he began to look back on the adventure as a bad dream. The day was sunny. The luxury hotel soothed his rattled nerves. He would make this his one drink, get some fishing, and try to lead a healthy life. The fees for fishing on the Anstey were steep, but he was a rich man. But one drink led to another and by the time he got to the river, he was unsteady on his feet.

Charlie, fishing downstream from Peter, looked along the sparkling peaty waters of the Anstey just in time to see Peter falling off the bank and into a salmon pool. He hurried along and pulled Peter out and dumped him on the bank. The smell of whisky coming off the man, thought Charlie, was polluting the very air. Charlie had the benefit of free fishing and the use of the hotel's Land Rover to get to the river. He heaved Peter up and, escorting him to the Land Rover, dumped him in the passenger seat, then drove back to the hotel. He found where Peter's room was and took him along. He stripped off his wet clothes and tossed them on the floor, got him into his pyjamas, and threw him on the bed.

Charlie was turning to leave when a mobile phone on the bedside table began to ring. Charlie picked it up and stared down at the number on the screen. Strathbane! He decided to answer it.

"This is Blair," snarled the familiar voice. "What have you found out?"

Charlie was a good mimic. He put on an upper-class English voice and said, "I've only just got here."

"You've had time enough, laddie," said Blair. "I want proof that the inspector was being bonked by Charlie Carter and I want it soonest or I'll have you."

Charlie sat down on a chair beside the bed, his superstitious highland soul telling him that he would never, ever get away with that night with Fiona.

He rose stiffly and went out into the hall and phoned Hamish, asking him to come quickly because Blair was on the warpath.

Then Charlie went out into the car park and waited for Hamish to arrive.

Hamish listened carefully to what Charlie had discovered. "Blast the man!" he said. "You'd better phone Fiona."

"I cannae!" wailed Charlie. "Every time I look at her, I see her with no clothes on."

"Some men have all the luck," said Hamish. "Phone her. She's got the clout to deal with this."

Miserably, Charlie phoned Inverness and told Fiona that Blair was trying to find out about their affair through some drunk called Peter Tuck. He obviously had some hold on him. "The man's a chronic drunk," said Charlie. "Maybe Blair let him off on a charge in return for spying."

"I'll see to it," said Fiona. "You'll hear from me later."

Blair was glad it was a quiet day. He had enjoyed a liquid lunch and was leaning back in his chair with his feet on his desk, his hands folded over his paunch, his eyes slowly closing.

His feet were suddenly swiped off the desk. He sat up, blinking his eyes, to see Daviot and Fiona looming over him. "My office. Now!" snapped Daviot.

Blair climbed up the stairs to Daviot's office, terror gripping him.

When they were seated, Fiona began. "There is a man called Peter Tuck, staying at the Tommel Castle Hotel, who has orders from you to find out if I had been having an affair with policeman Charlie Carter."

"He must be fantasising," said Blair. "As if I waud do such a thing."

"I have checked with the custody sergeant," said Fiona. "Last night you arrested this Mr. Tuck for being over the limit. He spent a night in the cells and was due in the sheriff's court this morning. The charges were dropped. His impounded car was returned to him and he was sent on his way. Why did you drop the charges?"

"We're overburdened with petty cases and the

court is overworked," said Blair sanctimoniously. "I made up my mind just to let him go."

"Your Mr. Tuck got drunk and fell in the river. Charlie Carter rescued him and put him to bed. While he was passed out, his mobile rang. Charlie answered it and it was you, Blair, and under the impression you were speaking to Tuck, you ordered him to find out if I was having an affair with Carter. What have you to say before I drag your fat carcase to court?"

"Oh, Inspector Herring," pleaded Daviot. "Think of the scandal. Blair, you are suspended from duty. Leave us."

Charlie and Hamish waited and waited at the hotel until Fiona arrived in the late evening. "Blair has been suspended though he should have been sacked," she said. "But I want this whole business buried as soon as possible. If Blair gets vindictive, he may hire a private detective. Now let's see Mr. Tuck."

Hamish was almost sorry for Peter as Fiona told him to pack up and leave for London or she would have him arrested on a number of charges. If he left immediately, no more would be said of the matter.

Babbling his thanks, Peter packed as quickly as possible, settled his bill, and roared off.

It was unfortunate that he stopped in a pub in Inverness to still his shaking nerves with several large drinks and even more unfortunate that he should buy a bottle of whisky for the car to refresh himself on his journey. It never really gets dark in the summer in the Highlands. Late in the evening, there is a sort of grey gloaming. It can trick the eyes, particularly the eyes of a very drunk man. South of Inverness, Peter was sure there was a woman in white standing in the middle of the road. He swerved violently and the Jaguar plunged off the road and rolled down and down, turning and turning and finally crashing into a great ice age boulder. Peter died in the crumpled wreck of his car.

"And that, in its way, is murder," said Hamish Macbeth. "If Blair had booked him and kept his car impounded, this would never have happened. Did Fiona leave all right, Charlie? Why did she want to see you in private?"

"Wanted to give me a proper goodbye," said Charlie, blushing to the roots of his hair. "But I couldnae. Herself was right angry. You haven't looked at your post."

"It's all junk these days," said Hamish, flipping through it. "Oh, what's this?"

He opened a stiff square envelope. Inside was an embossed card. It was an invitation to Dick and Anka's wedding.

Hamish handed it to Charlie and said bitterly, "I never will understand women. Wee Dick and gorgeous Anka! How did he do it?"

"Just being Dick," said Charlie. "He's sort of cosy."

"I'm beginning to think there'll never be a lassie for me," said Hamish.

When Charlie had left, Hamish sat turning the invitation over and over in his long fingers. Then he thought that he had never really seen beyond Anka's beauty.

He leaned down and patted Lugs and then Sally for comfort. "I'm done wi' beauty," he told them. "If a gorgeous female turns up on my doorstep, I'll tell her to take a hike."

He left the station and walked up to his favourite spot where the roaring Atlantic waves at the entrance to the loch pounded the cliffs. There was something mesmerising about the towering green-and-black waves, something about the noise and tumult which soothed his brain.

Back at the police station, he was just about to make a cup of coffee when there came a knock at the kitchen door. He opened it. Christine Dalray, the forensic scientist, stood there, her attractive face lit up in a smile. She was wearing a pretty, floaty summer dress, quite short, revealing her long, long legs to advantage.

"I'm back to sort out the mess in the lab at Strathbane," she said. "Do you know that despite the cleaning there was one hair lodged under the seat in Helen Mackenzie's car and the DNA was that of Harrison?"

"No, I didnae know that," said Hamish. "What a waste of an investigation."

"Never mind. I'm here to take you to dinner."

Hamish hesitated only a moment. "Grand," he said.

As he walked out of the station with her, Hamish noticed that Charlie had left an offering to the fairies.

"Do you believe in fairies?" he asked Christine.

"Not a bit of it. I've never even seen a ghost. Don't believe in them, either."

Little did Hamish Macbeth know that he was shortly to meet one as murder once more was due to return to his beat.